"THE BOUNTIFULL GYFTE"

A story of Dorset

Patricia M Wilnecker

By the same author:
non-fiction

High Street Murders 1598
Published by Poole Museum Service

A History of Upper Parkstone (beginning to 1939)
Upper Parkstone in the Second World War
More Recollections of Old Upper Parkstone
Published by Patricia M Wilnecker

Published by Patricia M Wilnecker
73 Gwynne Road
Parkstone
Poole, Dorset
BH12 2AR

First published 1991

British Library Cataloguing in Publication Data
Wilnecker, Pat
The Bountifull Gyfte: a story of Dorset
I. title
823.914

Typeset and printed in Great Britain by
Bourne Press Limited, Bournemouth

ISBN 0 9513971 3 3

To Joan Loader,
for her encouragement

CONTENTS

Preface

This story changed in the telling. The further I delved into the history of Purbeck the more incidents came to light, compelling me to include them. The *Bountifull Gyfte* was a real ship. William Drake, Meryatt, Hawley, Fox and Hatton as well as all the named pirates were real people and I have tried to portray them as factually as possible, although I admit to juggling the dates and sites a little to make events fit my story. Place names differ in some cases to the modern spelling but I have used the way they were written in Elizabethen times. (see footnote).

Many of the incidents, including that relating to the 'Salvator of Danzig' actually took place—as did the happening described in the prologue—they were cruel times.

Acknowledgements must go to 'A History of Poole' by H P Smith, Poole Borough Archives, 'Dorset Elizabethans at Home and Abroad,' by Rachel Lloyd, 'Christopher Hatton', by Eric St John Brooks, Poole Reference Library, Dorset County Record Office, Derek Beamish of the Poole Historical Trust and the good people of Purbeck, without whose assistance this book could not have been written.

I would like to say a special thank you to Robert Howard of 'Local History Magazine.' My books on the History of Upper Parkstone were published, and then he asked, "What are you going to do now?" This book is the result . . .

Prologue

In the cold light of a winter's day on Wednesday the 11th of February in the Year of Our Lord 1589 a ship was lying off the castle of Branksea, her topsail furled and mainsail hanging slack in the light breeze.

A young woman, standing on a gorse-covered sandbank by the rough track at North Haven point looked out across the harbour of Poole, watching as three men lowered a boat from the ship and rowed towards the castle.

'They are taking the permit ashore,' she thought. 'A pity, they may be some time,' and turned to walk back to the town, glancing over her shoulder every so often to see if they had returned.

She had not taken many paces when the creak of oars carried across the still harbour, and narrowing her eyes she squinted into the pale sunshine, trying to identify the oarsmen.

The three men reached the ship—it wasn't very far—and climbed back on board, the crew hastily making ready to sail.

Her mind wouldn't accept what happened next—like a small white cloud a puff of smoke issued from the castle, followed by the delayed crack of a sakre shot!

The women uttered a wordless cry, standing as though paralysed, hand pressed to her throat. Petrified, she watched as a distant figure on the ship removed his hat, waved it in the air and hailed his company.

"Hoist the main topsail!" he commanded, and the rattle of wooden parrels as they slid up the mast echoed across the water to her straining ears while the crew hurried about their business.

The gunner, seeing his first shot had missed, fired off a

second sakre which he levelled between wind and water. The shot fell short, skimming over the sea like a stone and bounced, striking the ship at deck level.

Two men fell mortally wounded, and for a tense moment there was deathly silence, until terrifyingly their agonised cries carried across the water.

The woman gave an anguished moan—"Oh my Steven—my love, please God NO, not my Steven!"

Slowly, very slowly the ship came about and headed back to port, whilst on shore the woman ran towards Poole on leaden feet, her breath coming in painful gasps, tears coursing unheeded down her cheeks . . .

CHAPTER 1

Sarah Trinity

The autumn morning was still and frosty. Mist drawn up by the sun curled from the surface of the sea and through it, briefly, a skein of geese appeared honking their way from Branksea Island over the water to the mainland of Poole.

Sarah Trinity ran along the quayside lifting her brown fustian skirts to leap over the frozen puddles, fair curls bouncing on her white collar.

"I've stayed too long again," she chided herself, "and that'll mean trouble!" But she loved to watch the ships, and on her way back from the market had been drawn irresistibly to the quay. Following the course of a vessel as it slowly sailed into port, spellbound she watched the master skilfully capturing every light breath of wind, and now the tall masts stood like winter trees bare of leaves, rigging taut in the still air.

High on the spars of one such barque, busily furling sails, a mariner saw her out of the corner of his eye and called a greeting. "You should 'ave been a lad, me gurl—the way you run!" he joked. "Why don't you sail wi' us next week—as cabin boy?"

She paused for a moment waving gaily up at him, calling breathlessly, "Oh Tom, I'd love to and you know it! But I daren't stop. I lose track of time when I'm here and I'm late with the butter already—my aunt will clout me again!" Her flying figure was familiar to the mariners, and her merry eyes and quick smile cheered many a heart homesick for their own children.

The town, with its houses of wealthy merchants and ordinary working folk, lay on a spit of land in the largest natural harbour in the western world. To the south were the rolling Purbeck hills and surrounding the town was the great heath. At the western end of the harbour lay the old Saxon town of Wareham, once a busier port than Poole until the river silted up, and from there the sparse forest of birch and conifer stretched to the village of Corfe with its stately castle. In the harbour were its five jewels—the islands of Branksea, Fursey, St Helen's, Long and Round, but Sarah had no time to spare to admire them now.

Reaching the end of the quay she ran through the archway, heart pounding, past Paradise Cellars where a friendly mongrel joined her, running alongside and barking merrily, coming at last to the stone house near the church where her aunt lived. Hurrying across the courtyard to the kitchens she hoped fervently that she hadn't been missed.

The warmth from the room was welcoming as, swinging open the heavy oaken door an appetising smell wafted from the pots on the fire, the draught blowing a fine coating of ash down the chimney and into the room.

"So you decided to come back—you really do be the limit! Cut that bread and spread the butter or the fish'll be spoiled. You be in luck me gurl, your aunt 'as a visitor and 'asn't missed you yet." Joan the cook was a comfortably built, homely soul in her thirties with an elusive tendril of hair that always seemed to be escaping from her cap, and with kind eyes set above the red rosy cheeks of someone whose life has been spent near the stove. In spite of her sharp words she was fond of the girl, cushioning her when she could from the attention of her harsh aunt.

"Well, what ships were in?" she asked, giving her a kindly smile, guessing that Sarah had returned by way of the quay as usual. She was making the pastry for a fish pie, and rolled the mixture deftly on a smooth marble slab as she spoke. "The drays were clattering over the cobbles, so one must've come in this morning." The cook loved to hear what was happening in the town and indeed there wasn't much that went on without her knowing it.

Sarah smiled a wistful smile, seeing the ships in her mind's eye. "There was the *Anne of Plymouth*, the *Prymrose* and—oh Joan, my favourite barque—Master Meryatt's *Bountifull Gyfte*. Tom Jolliffe was aloft in the rigging and asked me if I'd like to sail with them." Her green eyes dreamy, she spread the butter saying, "I KNOW he was only joking, but wouldn't it be wonderful to be a lad and sail off on adventures?"

"Aye, and be sea-sick, get scurvy, feel a cat-o-nine-tails, be 'alf-frozen and soaked most of the time, get captured by pirates and probably sink, so there!" said the ever-practical Joan. "Very exciting I'm sure!" firmly putting an end to the conversation. Tossing back the elusive strand of hair, she smeared her forehead with flour and they prepared the rest of the meal in a companionable silence, broken only by the sound of voices in the hallway and the front door opening and closing as the visitor departed.

Sarah had been born in Sturminster, a small village of thatched cob cottages a few miles to the north, but since the death of her parents in an epidemic one harsh winter when she was ten years old, lived for the past five years with her aunt, a strict, unloving spinster, earning her keep by helping with the housework and the cooking.

The girl smiled to herself and hummed a little tune, her thoughts still with the ships at the quayside as she completed the preparations for the noon meal. In spite of the harsh upbringing she had a happy nature and was popular with the seafaring lads of the port. With her slim, boyish figure they treated her as one of themselves and teased her good humouredly about her dreams of adventure, but indeed life in Poole in those days of Good Queen Bess was pretty turbulent. There was fear of invasion by the Spanish, and lawlessness abounded while piracy was rife and a hazard to honest mariners.

"Sarah—come here!" her aunt's stern voice called from the solar, interrupting her reverie. Wiping her hands and straightening her apron Sarah hastened to her bidding, wondering what she had done now!

Crossing the hallway she knocked on the door then entered the solar, a room panelled in dark oak with a window looking out on to a formal garden stiff with an early frost, and turned apprehensively to face her aunt who was seated straight backed before the fire.

"Yes aunt?" she murmured dutifully.

The woman looked her up and down before replying. She saw a slim, bubbly child on the threshold of womanhood who would be a beauty some day soon. Her most arresting features were her strange tawny/green eyes with their fathomless expression—far too precocious for her years—and her small, heart shaped face. Yes, she was a potential pocketful of trouble—something SHE was not prepared to deal with, and fate had just given her an opportunity of ridding herself of the burden.

"I have been called to London. My uncle—your great uncle—is ill and not expected to live. I am to inherit his house and will be going there immediately to take charge. I will be very busy and have not time for a child, therefore you are to go to my cousin in Purbeck."

This was shattering news—a bolt from the blue! The room seemed to tilt and whirl about her and swallowing she said in a small voice, "For how long, aunt?"

"For good! London is no place for a growing girl and I have had your responsibility for long enough!"

Sarah's cheeks paled but she stuck out her chin bravely. To be cast off like this, even though the old woman had shown her little affection over the years and made no attempt to hide the fact that she was kept on out of a sense of duty, certainly not love! Very well, she would go to Purbeck and try to make a life for herself and NEVER let anyone hurt her again! The shock had made her dizzy and putting out a hand to steady herself, attempted to hide her emotions, not wanting to give the old woman the satisfaction of knowing she was upset.

"What will happen to the house—and Joan?"

"I shall sell the house and Joan can find another employment. Be ready to leave on Monday."

That gave her two days to get used to the idea and reorganise her life.

* * *

On board the barque moored at the quayside there was a bustle of activity. Men called to each other as they unshipped the cargo, happy to have a few days shore leave ahead of them. The *Bountifull Gyfte*, a trim three masted ship carried goods from the continent and between the coastal ports. These were difficult times on the seas. Pirates abounded in the troubled waters around England and to defend herself against them and the Spanish she carried two small cannon. She was eighty feet long and conditions on board for the crew were cramped, but this was commonplace for Elizabethan ships. However, she was a fine, seaworthy ship, well able to cope with the stormy conditions often to be found around the rocky coast of the south west.

Steven Curnow's sea-grey eyes swept over the vessel. A Cornishman by birth, the sea was his element. His leather tunic, kneebreeches and sea-boots were marbled with salt water stains, and his face throat and arms brown from exposure to all weathers. He and his fellow mariners worked in harmony, putting the sails into their harbour-furl, making the ship secure at the end of the voyage and unloading the cargo. Now the tasks were finished and there were a few welcome days to call their own before the next voyage.

On the bridge, Walter Meryatt the ship's master glanced up as he was joined by the mate William Drake. The pair had long been friends and shared many a hazardous voyage together.

"Looks like a fair evening," he reflected, peering into the frosty sky and casting an eye at the clouds on the horizon, "but I'd say there will be a bit of a blow coming up the channel before long." Emphasizing the point he pulled his hat on more firmly and sniffed the air—a real 'sea dog'. "Still, we're prepared—everything's battened down and safely stowed away. Got a good price for the cargo, too," he added contentedly.

For a while the pair stood watching the ships, until a puff of wind wafted the smell of fish to them from nets hanging to dry on the fishermans quay. Reminded of his empty stomach and the meal his goodwife would have ready, Meryatt gave a contented sigh.

"Well, that's another voyage done. Will you join me and the family in our evening meal tonight?"

"Tomorrow perhaps," replied Drake, stretching, and stroking his pointed beard. "I've a mind to be with my folks this evening. The youngest child won't go to bed until she sees what I have brought her," and laughing together the pair went ashore, arms on each others shoulders, calling greetings to passers-by on the quay as they went for they were popular figures in the town.

Steven, his tasks finished swung himself on land. He had changed out of his salt-stained sea clothes into a clean shirt, jerkin and breeches, his thick springing curls tamed momentarily by a damp comb and his fringe beard neatly trimmed close to his chin. Walking along the quay he noticed Sarah standing alongside, scuffing her toes against a bollard.

"What's wrong, lass," he called, seeing her woebegone face. "This isn't like you, moppet—tears?"

She had been hoping to see him. He was tall, strong and friendly and quite unbeknown to him, in her dull, uneventful life he was her hero and she spun imaginary adventures around him to herself.

"Oh Steve, I'm to go away on Monday for good, to Purbeck!" The whole sorry story poured out, her thin shoulders shaking with emotion.

Putting a finger under her chin he tilted her head back so she had to look up at him, eyes awash. "You poor little soul!" he said gently. "But sweeting, you always wanted adventure! Who's to know what will happen in Purbeck? Look on the bright side and don't worry little girl, you're a survivor if ever I saw one—you'll manage all right! Come on now, cut along home, there's a good lass." He realised he would miss her dog-like devotion and usually cheerful presence on the quay, almost like a younger brother! Which reminded him, his own young cousin Ben was waiting for him at the tavern. Ruffling her hair affectionately he promptly forgot her and went in search of Ben, leaving the disconsolate girl alone on the quayside.

Dusk was falling as he walked briskly away, his breath clouding before him in the chill evening air as one by one the stars appeared in the clear night sky.

She stayed awhile watching the ghostly forms of

wheeling herring gulls against the black velvet of the sea, their raucous voices silent now with the coming of nightfall, then reluctantly turned her steps for perhaps the last time towards what she had come to know as home.

* * *

Monday morning's cold light filtered under the tiles of Sarah's attic bedroom. The sun was shining fitfully between the clouds which, as foretold by the master of the *Bountifull Gyfte* had brought showers along the channel for the past couple of days but now were blown away to the east. Gulls calling on the roof roused her from her sleep and, her customary good humour restored, rubbed her eyes and stretched, greeting the new day with a smile. Her mind was made up, she would take Steven's advice and look on the bright side—today was going to be different—she was going to Purbeck and a new life! Her aunt's cousin, Richard Bonville farmed at Worth, near St Aldhelm's Head. She had never been there but had heard talk of it, so in spite of everything it was exciting to think of the prospect of being in the high, windswept hills with their views of the sea.

Throwing back the old, worn blanket she swung her bare legs over the side of the bed and stood up. Shivering, she pulled off her flannel nightgown and splashed herself with cold water from the dented pewter bowl on the table which, apart from the bed was the only furniture in the little room. Goose bumps covered her limbs as, teeth chattering she dried her body with the rough cloth that served as a towel and dressed quickly, putting on a green woollen dress over her plain chemise.

Humming the popular tune 'Greensleeves' and pulling a comb through her fair curls she mentally ticked off her instructions. Her aunt was leaving by the early carrier. When she had seen her off she was to take the Passage boat across the harbour to Ower Quay, travel by the local carrier's cart through the village of Corfe and over the Purbeck hills to the farm.

Hurrying downstairs she dashed through her morning

chores then, excited at the prospect of being afloat began preparing breakfast for the old woman. The last time I shall be doing this, she thought to herself.

A cry disturbed her daydreams as her aunt came in. The girl hadn't seen it in her preoccupation but the kitchen cat had crept on to the table, about to steal some bread.

"You careless wench!" screamed the old woman boxing her about the ears as it shot out of the way, "I can't trust you for a minute—you are good for nothing! I don't know why I kept you here for so long. Have you packed my trunk or have you forgotten that too?"

"It's all ready aunt. I prepared it before breakfast," Sarah answered, ignoring the stinging pain and pleased at having done the right thing for once. That'll be the last time she boxes my ears anyway, she thought to herself.

"I leave at nine of the clock," said the old woman thanklessly. Tight-lipped, with a disapproving look on her hawk-like features she turned instead to Joan, stating "I have an inventory of everything that is in the house. Master Cloade has a copy and will be sending my goods on to me by carrier. He is seeing to the sale of the house so don't you think you can rob me of anything!" and rising from the table she collected her cloak from a chair.

Phew! You daft old biddy, thought Joan silently, I wouldn't want yer rotten ole rubbish anyhow!

"Fetch my trunk, girl!" ordered the old woman and Sarah hurried through the kitchen to collect it.

Catching her arm, Joan gave her an impulsive hug, realising she would be amongst strangers at the farm and would have no-one there to befriend her. "I'll think of you often, lass!"

"Oh Joan," whispered Sarah, "I WILL miss you!" and they clung together, aware of the unspoken affection there was between them and not knowing if they would ever meet again.

The motherly soul gave her another squeeze then pushing her away gently said, "Be off, before the old dragon's chasing you!"

Sarah staggered back with her aunt's heavy trunk, her young shoulders bent with the weight. Resting it against the wall she found the door was latched and as she struggled to open it the trunk slipped from her hands with a crash.

Quickly intervening, seeing her mistress about to burst with rage Joan cried, "Oh ma'am, 'tis too 'eavy for the girl. If I takes one end and she t'other we'll carry it safely between us."

For once the old woman agreed without argument. "Very well, but make haste about it or I will miss the carrier."

"That'd NEVER do!" muttered Joan.

Fastening her travelling cloak around her shoulders the old woman swept out of the house, leading the way to the stables across the street, leaving Sarah and Joan struggling along with the trunk, trying to avoid the mud and puddles from the overnight rain. Glancing at each other they exchanged conspiratorial grins at having for once got the better of the old woman.

"Good riddance, says I!" Joan whispered under her breath.

The carrier was waiting, horses groomed and champing at the bit, ready to go. Taking her position aboard the cart the old woman settled herself in the best seat whilst the driver, groaning at the weight, heaved the trunk aboard.

"Hurry now Sarah, the Passage boat will not wait. Remember me to my cousin and behave yourself," and with no fond word of farewell or backward glance Sarah's aunt went out of her life . . .

* * *

The girl hurried back to the house, took a last look around and collecting her few belongings together made her way to the quay, chin held high and biting her lip to hold back the tears, for the old woman when all was said and done was her closest living relative, her only contact with the past and now she was entirely on her own.

Goodbye house, she thought silently, Goodbye ships. Will I ever see you again? This is it, I'm on my own now. Then, taking a deep breath, she faced the future.

The Passage boat was waiting at the ferry steps. It was

not very large, having only one sail and two pairs of oars. The ferryman and his son made the round trip daily, weather permitting. Taking the girl's bundle the younger man stowed it away at the bow of the boat and Sarah found herself a seat.

Joan came to see her off and squeezed her hand, waving once, calling, "Be good—but be 'appy!" and wiping her eyes with her apron turned and retraced her steps to the house by the church, heaving a sigh of relief that she was free of the old dragon! She had found herself another place as cook in Master Cloade's household and he promised to be far more tolerant than the old woman. She had only stayed on for the girl's sake, poor motherless child that she was, and now she was off into the unknown and on the threshold of womanhood.

Sarah, her happy nature unable to be squashed for long, was in spite of everything quietly bubbling with excitement. She settled herself in the boat wedged between a goat and a cage containing live chickens but she didn't mind—she was afloat!

The sun was dancing on the water as the ferryman's son cast off and the creak of the oars in the thole-pins was music to her ears. Looking hopefully for Steven as they passed the *Bountifull Gyfte* she saw the ship was deserted and all hands ashore. However, even that couldn't dull her pleasure as, rounding the point of Ham they headed out across the harbour. The breeze was quite strong but as yet the water wasn't very choppy. She remembered the mariners lore which Steven had taught her, 'When the wind comes before the waves it won't last long, but when the waves come before the wind—we're in for a long blow.'

The long tawny length of Branksea island with its sandy beaches and scrubby heather clad slopes grew larger as they drew close, but they sailed past, leaving it on their port side. Passing the smaller islands of Fursey and St Helen's which were joined together in those days by a bridge they bobbed, heading south to the mainland of Purbeck.

Sarah breathed deeply, fresh salty air heady as wine as she lay back, nothing to do for once, experiencing the exhilaration of new sensations—the gentle rocking of the boat, the wind on her face and in the sail, salt spray on her cheeks and the creak and dip, dip of the oars as the boatmen made their way across the harbour.

Gazing around with interest she saw cormorants resting on a sandbank spreading their wings bat-like to dry, whilst nearer to the shore a small flock of black and white oyster-catchers flew away, uttering their plaintive calls of alarm as the boat approached the inlet leading to Ower Quay. 'Quay' was a rather grandiose term for the scattering of cottages and a little pottery that surrounded the small jetty, but it was the point where stone from the Purbeck quarries was transported and also the main landing place in that part of the harbour which elsewhere was full of reeds and salt flats.

Scrambling ashore the passengers passed their goods out on to the jetty. Relieved to be back on dry land the goat bleated and broke away from his owner, leading him a merry chase. The man almost caught the rope, calling "Dang the beast!" as it eluded him, then slipping on a patch of mud measured his length on the ground and Sarah chuckled to herself at their antics as the animal scampered away. She and another passenger managed to corner it when, pausing, it ate from a bush and the owner reclaimed his beast with an embarrassed grin and a muttered thanks.

The ferryman's son helped her with her bag. "Here y'are m'girl. 'Tidn't very heavy, you 'adn't got much in yer, 'ave you?" and carried it to the start of the track where the carrier was waiting.

His cart with four great wheels was drawn by two sturdy horses standing patiently, tossing their heads to ward off the flies, as the sun had come out now and there were a few dozy ones left on this autumn day. Calling to Sarah he cried, "Come on lass, climb up here alongside me. You'll get a good view and be out of the mud."

Giving him a quick smile, Sarah swung herself up on to the seat and thanked him. He was an old man but he was delighted to have this pretty young thing sitting next to him, and seeing her interest and discovering that she hadn't been there before pointed out the sights along the way.

There was still a trace of colour in the heather, whilst the bracken had turned to yellow and gold. On either side hedgerows were fringed with hawthorn berries, elderberries and 'old mans beard' which gleamed like hoarfrost in the sunshine as they made slow progress along the bumpy, potholed track, gradually leaving the harbour and heatherlands behind them.

Topping a rise, the carrier pointed to a gap in the range of chalk hills. "Look, straight ahead." There was a smaller hill in the gap and crowning it was the imposing castle of Corfe.

Sarah gasped with pleasure. "I've never seen it as close as this!" She had seen it in the distance from across the harbour in Poole of course, but close-to it was spectacular, with pale grey towers reaching to the sky from their surrounding walls, gleaming in the late autumn sunshine.

The bumpy road skirted the castle and passed through Corfe village, a cluster of stone cottages around the little church, some thatched and others with stone roofs—large tiles at the bottom, gradually getting smaller as they reached the ridge, distributing the immense weight on the beams below; their sheltered gardens bright with flowers and herbs that had survived the recent frost.

"Whoa boys!" called the carter, pulling on the reins and drawing his team to a halt by a stone trough filled with water. Turning round to Sarah he explained, "We must give them a rest before the haul up Afflington Hill, so you've time to stretch your legs and have a bite to eat at the inn if you so desire."

The fresh air had given Sarah an appetite and her stomach was rumbling noisily, but she didn't have a penny to her name, so dismounting she stood hesitantly and unsure of herself outside the inn.

You fool, the carrier told himself, the child can't afford anything! Giving her a wave he called, "Here, lass, come and have some of this bread and cheese. My good woman has given me more than enough and I've a flagon of ale too if you be thirsty."

"You are very kind, I AM hungry but didn't think to bring anything for myself," and she gratefully took the food from him, sitting on the bench outside the inn and stretched her toes in the meagre warmth of the pale sun, watching the customers coming and going. Men and women stood in the doorway talking of ailments, recipes and crops; who was to be wed and who was with child. Joan would have enjoyed this, she thought and suffered a momentary pang of loneliness.

The horses were rested and they continued their journey. Afflington Hill was very steep and rough so they walked alongside the great beasts to lighten their load, supplementing their snack by gathering and eating the blackberries which grew alongside the track as they went. Pheasants ran off into the brambles and others shot up into the air with their 'UUK-UUK' cries of alarm, disturbed by their passage. Curious sheep gathered by the roadside, watching as they approached, then courage failing and ears flattened they fled away bleating noisily.

Rocks littered the road giving the cart a very bumpy ride as it followed the line of the scarp and, stopping along the way at isolated farmsteads and at cottages in the hamlet of Hill Bottom they made deliveries; to one, a bale of material, to another a pot which had been repaired, and so on up the steep hill to Renscombe until they turned towards Worth.

Sarah's face glowed from the fresh air reminding her of the days of her childhood in the fields at home. At last, as the sky flamed in the west in a glorious sunset they came to the Bonville farmhouse and drew to a halt.

"Here we are, journey's end lass," said the carrier and climbing out of the waggon Sarah stood looking around her. She had to admit it was a beautiful sight. The old stone farm with its lichen covered roof had weathered many a storm, and it clung to the hillside with house and outbuildings hugging the contours as though they had grown there. A circular dovecote stood in the yard and the fat, slumbrous cooing of its inhabitants filled the evening air. Away in a vee at the bottom of the green valley lay the sea, catching the colour of the setting sun. Birds called to each other and after the jolting of the cart it seemed very peaceful.

The friendly carrier off-loaded her bag, waved goodbye, shook the reins and drove off with his patient, plodding horses leaving Sarah feeling she was severing the last connection with her childhood.

"I shall make the best of it," she told herself firmly, remembering Steven's advice.

As the creaking of cartwheels died away Richard Bonville came to the stone porch which shielded the door of the farm and a cat shot out, heading for the barn and mice. A dark, stockily built man with the strong shoulders of one who was used to working in the open, he stood with one hand resting on the door jamb, looking at Sarah speculatively.

"So you've arrived. Come inside and shut the door, the heat from the fire is being wasted," and went back into the farmhouse.

Well—not much of a welcome! she thought.

"Hello, pretty wench," said a voice from the porch. "You will be wanting a hand with that baggage . . .?"

Sarah turned and saw a thin, ruddy faced man with lank hair wearing a dirty thigh-length tunic. His piggy eyes leered at her making the blood rush to her cheeks, and he said suggestively, "You an' me'll have a fine old time, won't we, my pretty?" The fellow was Melchoir Strangeways, a peasant who amongst other things worked on the farm for the Bonvilles.

Sarah stepped back in revulsion, startled, her chin tilted and drew herself up the full height of her fifteen years. "I can manage myself, thank you!" she said and started to carry her bag inside.

"Oh I see, Miss 'oity-Toity is it, not good enough fer you b'aint I?" said the peasant making a grab at her arm.

Cheeks aflame now with embarrassment she shook him off, saying "I'll thank you to leave me alone. I'm here at the invitation of your master and I trust you will remember that. I'm no wanton!" but her lip was trembling at the fellow's words. She had just arrived and had made an enemy already! Turning away before he could see how upset she was, she left the yokel standing on the doorstep, scowling with rage.

"No chit of a girl treats me like that," he muttered to himself. "I'll repay her, see if I don't!"

* * *

One thing that could be said in her favour—perhaps the only thing—was that Mistress Bonville made excellent pies. Her fame as a pie-maker had spread throughout Purbeck and although her husband was a small scale landowner he didn't consider himself 'gentry' and did not expect his wife to be either. Therefore he had no objections when she told him she would be selling pies to other Purbeck folk, but in other respects she differed very little from Sarah's aunt. Childless herself, she had no love for the girl. She had not wanted her to come there but her husband had said the extra pair of hands would be useful and the girl would not need paying.

One of Sarah's tasks—as well as cooking, helping in the house and feeding the hens and cows—was to deliver the pies. She welcomed the escape from drudgery and soon found her way around. It was hardly possible to get lost, all she had to do was keep the sea to the south and the chalk hills to the north and she could find her way anywhere. Sandwyche was east and Corfe west although she had not ventured into the villages yet, the customers were either in outlying cottages or quarry workers.

One day in late spring she set out to deliver a pie to Mother Wellman at Seacombe Cottage. She carried a piece of bread and cheese wrapped up in a cloth to eat on the way as it was late morning before she could set out, having seen to the milch-cows and chickens earlier.

The air was so still, not a breath of wind, that all she could hear was the baa-ing of a lamb calling for its mother on the opposite side of the valley, and the thumping of her heart as she climbed the steep path. Sitting for a while to regain her breath she rested on a cracked boulder abandoned by the quarrymen and listened to the stillness. It was so quiet she could hear the sheep cropping the grass, and one by one, growing curious they gathered around her in a semi-circle staring at her with their peculiar eyes.

Laughing, she said. "You silly woolly-heads, I'm not going to do anything!" and gradually losing interest they returned to their grazing.

From high in the blue came the rejoicing of a lark, soaring aloft, pouring out its heart in song. Producing her bread and cheese she shared it with some cheeky sparrows who appeared as if by magic at the sight of food. Peeling a wrinkled apple in one piece she threw the peel over her left shoulder to see who her lover would be, smiling secretly to herself when it formed an 'S'. Then, lying back on the boulder she watched the clouds forming towering castles and chewed on a piece of grass, enjoying the brief freedom and the sunshine . . . What was that? Seeing a flicker out of the corner of her eye she shielded them from the sun and glanced upwards. Yes, it was a kestrel hovering over its prey, completely steady in the still air—then it stooped into the withy bed by a little stream and was lost to sight.

A cloud passed over the sun, bringing her back to the present and her responsibilities. Sighing, she climbed down from the boulder, brushing her skirt and went on down the path, disturbing a brimstone butterfly which flew away like a primrose on the wing. White tails bobbed as rabbits slipped into the gorse as she passed, until turning the final corner before the sea she reached the cottage at last.

Mother Wellman, a wizened little old woman came to the door. "'Ello my dear, got my pie 'ave yer? I bin lookin' forward to 'ee! Come along in, wont yer?"

"I mustn't stop long Mother, I've been dallying on the way. T'was so peaceful in the valley, I've never known it so still."

"Arr, can be sometimes . . . 'tis sheltered yer. I did see they sea-parrots this mornin', comin' in off the sea with lots o' liddle fishes in their beaks, all at once. Funny liddle souls . . . I likes to see 'em. There, wot am I thinkin' of! Will 'ee have a sup wi' me?"

"Sorry Mother, I really must be going. I've more pies to deliver yet at Renscombe. I'll see you again next week."

"Thank 'ee lass, t'is lovely to see a young face 'cos I gets proper lonesome yer sometimes. Yor a good gurl."

Sarah waved farewell and took the other arm of the

valley past ancient drystone walls. It always seemed full of birds, reminding her of her childhood and the woods by the strange old earthworks of Spetisbury Rings, a magical place. She supposed it was lonely, but SHE never felt alone there.

And so time passed. Month followed uneventful month and season followed uneventful season. "Will my life ALWAYS be like this?" she asked herself, sighing for adventure . . .

CHAPTER 2

The Meryatt's

Another voyage over and the *Bountifull Gyfte* was in her home port again.

Bidding his mate goodnight, Walter Meryatt made his way homewards. He didn't live far from the quay, in fact from his attic window he could see the masts and spars of ships at the quayside.

As he walked, his mind ran back over the voyage just completed. They had been across to Jersey—a short trip this time—and brought back a cargo of canvas and linen. He had a good crew, most of whom had been with him for some years.

"Young Curnow is doing all right," he mused, visualising his crew-member. "Tall for a Cornishman, broad-shouldered, pleasant manners and features, keeps himself clean, hair and beard tidy,"—he liked his mariners to be fastidious, it went with a trim ship—"although I sense he's keeping something hidden. Still, that's his own business, as long as it doesn't interfere with the running of my ship or cause trouble. He's a good seaman, reliable and cool in an emergency." His train of thought was interrupted by a greeting from a passer by. Doffing his hat and exchanging greetings he went on his way.

Meryatt was a family man and ignored the pull of inns and alehouses at the end of a voyage, content to rejoin the bosom and comfort of his family. That was not to say that he disliked taverns—but they could wait for another day.

By then he had reached his door. It opened wide and a small boy shot out.

"Father! Father—you're home! How was the voyage? How much longer must I wait before I go with you?"

Meryatt smiled benevolently, swinging the child up in his arms.

"Willy, my lad, it's good to see you! Where's your mother?

"In the kitchen getting your food ready. It's roast beef!" and as he spoke the appetising smell wafted to greet his father.

"Walter!" Mistress Meryatt appeared in the passage, kissing her husband's cheek, a sparkle in her eyes. "It's good to have you home safely, my love." She was a handsome woman, tall, straight backed but curved in the right places—like a ship, he thought bestowing on her the highest compliment he could. He held her at arms length for a moment, admiring her, then engulfed her in a bear-like hug.

"It's good to be back! We had an easy run this time. The winds were in our favour and we picked up our cargo without any delays."

He crossed the room to the corner where a boy of eighteen months was asleep on the settle, head pillowed on a cushion.

"And how is my babe?"

"Poor lamb, he couldn't go to bed until you came home. When Clement Starre called to say the *Bountifull Gyfte* was coming past the Cales—he'd been fishing there—the child was so excited he wore himself out. Getting advance warning meant I could roast the beef, though!"

"It smells delicious!"

"Draw up the stools Willy, and we will eat."

The baby woke as Willy dragged and scraped the stools across the stone-flagged floor. Rubbing his eyes sleepily he looked up, a beautiful smile lighting his little face and cried "Dadda!"

Sliding off the settle he toddled across to his father who lifted him proudly on to his lap where he dandled him, singing "Too-roo ricknock ricknock ricknock, too-roo ricknock ricknock norum," to the delighted chuckles of the child.

The family ate their meal in the soft glow of an oil lamp, Walter doing justice to the beef.

"You're a grand cook," he said smiling at his wife. "It's a welcome thought at the end of a voyage knowing I have all this to come home to."

When they had done, Willy helped his mother clear the table then the family sat around the fire together, the baby on his mother's knee and Willy next to his father on the settle.

"Tell me 'bout the voyage, father. Were the seas rough? What cargo did you bring back?" He yawned, fighting to keep his eyes open.

His father smiled proudly. "Come on, up to bed," he said kindly. "When you're tucked in I'll tell you all about it." Lighting a candle with a spill from the fire he took the lad by the hand and led him up the wooden stairs.

"But baby's not in bed yet!" he protested.

"He had a sleep earlier. I will carry him up when we've had our chat together. Come on lad, crew don't argue with the Master!"

"Aye aye sir!" piped Willy climbing into bed and dropping off to sleep in the middle of another question almost as soon as his head touched the pillow.

* * *

Walter and his wife, alone at last sat by the fire.

"Was it REALLY a good trip—no trouble with pirates? They are becoming an awful hazard, no-one is safe. I was at the market yesterday my love, and they were saying awful things."

"Don't you listen to 'em lass! They'd have a job to catch the *Bountifull Gyfte*, she'd show any of 'em a clean pair of heels! Anyhow, we weren't bothered by 'em." He had seen them anchored in Studland bay though, and had made a wide sweep to avoid them—but no sense in worrying the woman!

They sat in a companionable silence as the glowing logs settled in the grate, Walter drawing on his tobacco pipe which he had taken to smoking recently.

"Well," he said after a while, "will you be going to the fair at Woodberry Hill this year?"

"Oh Walter—it's held this week! Could . . . could you spare the time to come with us?

He squeezed her shoulders. "And why wouldn't I? With

the prettiest Goodwife in all of Dorset by my side and money to spend—we'll go tomorrow!"

Her cheeks flushed with pleasure.

"You're SO good to me Walter. I'm a lucky woman. Well, we'd best get up to bed then, if we've a long day ahead of us tomorrow." She dimpled at him, "That is—if you've a mind?"

He threw back his head and laughed.

"By God, you've a way with you, my girl—come on!" and mounting the stairs two at a time led her to their bed-chamber.

* * *

It was a clear and bright morning and the sun peeping in at the east-facing windows of the children's room woke them from their slumbers. They played together until their mother came in.

"Come on boys, let's get you dressed," she said happily. "Your father is taking us to the fair at Woodberry Hill."

"Hurray!" yelled Willy.

"'Ray, 'ray!" echoed his brother, not understanding but wanting to be included and they were dressed in record time, soon sitting at the scrubbed table eating their bread and milk together.

Walter, an early riser had been out and borrowed a neighbour's horse and cart for the day, and it stood waiting outside the door.

"Come along, quickly with your breakfast," called their mother.

Before very long the family was seated in the cart, ready for their outing. Mistress Meryatt had prepared a basket of food for their noon meal and it was wrapped in a cloth to keep the pasties fresh.

"Cast off amidships!" called Walter, pretending they were on a ship.

"Cast off, sir!" answered Willy. This was a great game!

They made their way through the town and out of the gates into the countryside where people were driving their cattle on to Long Flete heath to graze. The horse trotted along at a good pace, around Lytchett bay, an inlet of the harbour, picking its way carefully through the muddy patches then making up time again across the heath to Bloxworth, where they met more and more people converging on the elm lined wide dusty track to Woodberry Hill.

It was a big fair, the most important in the south of England and had been held on the ten acre ancient earthwork since the time of Henry III. The fair lasted for five days—Wholesale Day, Gentlefolk's Day which was given up largely to amusements, with feasting on roast pork and oysters, Allfolk's Day, Sheep Fair Day where the woolly beasts bleated in hurdled pens awaiting their fate, and Pack and Penny Day, when unsold goods were disposed of cheaply.

It was also a Hiring Fair where people looking for work hired their services to the highest bidders, each group of workers carrying the mark of their trade—a crook or tuft of wool for a shepherd, straw for a cowman, a whip for a carter and a mop for a maid.

Today was Allfolk's Day, and young Willy had never seen so many people gathered together in one place in all his short life. He was fascinated by glimpses of the fire eaters, jugglers, cheap-jacks, toy peddlars, booths decorated with ribbons and furbelows, dancing bears, sweetmeat and pastry vendors, horses, pigs, cattle, jackets, dresses—and just about everything you could imagine for sale or to be entertained by. He jigged from foot to foot in an agony of impatience whilst his father secured the horse's nosebag, having released it from the cart and tethered it with the other horses to rest until the journey home.

"Come on then," said Walter, swinging his youngest son on to his shoulders out of the press of the crowd, and the family feasted their eyes on the wares, wandering from attraction to attraction.

Willy suddenly stopped in his tracks, his eyes round with wonder and was swallowed up in the mass of people. His parents, missing him searched frantically in the throng, calling his name over and over again. Then at last Walter found him standing entranced at the last stall, not even realising he had been missed.

"Willy," said his father, exasperated. "You MUST keep with us of you'll get lost," then saw what the boy was gazing at. There, on a booth was a model ship complete in every detail–rigging, decks, spars, sails–everything! The child stood there spellbound.

Walter and his wife exchanged glances. He raised his eyebrows and she, reading his mind nodded with a smile.

"You'd like that, wouldn't you, son?" he said.

"Oh, father–a ship of my own–I WOULD!" his eyes shining.

"Well, I suppose I'd better buy it then!"

"Oh THANK YOU, thank you! You are the best father I've ever had!"

His parents roared with laughter and bought the little ship, placing it in the lad's outstretched hands.

"Now she is delicate – I don't have to tell you to be careful with her, do I?"

"I shall guard her with my life, father," said the child solemnly.

There was a sudden commotion and everyone looked to see what was happening. A horse came by with a man walking in front beating a drum. Sitting on the horse facing its rear was a man with a tankard tied around his neck and a bunch of pewter measures dangling from the animal's tail. Following behind was a crowd of jeering lads, cat-calling and yelling names.

"What is it, father?" cried Willy, alarmed.

He laughed. "He's a tippler who has repeatedly given short measure, lad. He'll be more careful next time!" The boy gazed after him, fascinated by the punishment.

They walked on around the fair, amused by the entertainers and came at last to the mercers booths. Walter caught his wife looking longingly at a red ossett petticoat.

"Would you like that, my love?" he asked.

She looked at him demurely.

"It's beautiful, but RED–isn't it a bit . . . well . . . WANTON?"

"Do you LIKE it?" he repeated.

Giving him a shy smile – a young girl again – she said "Do you know, my love, I've always yearned for a red ossett petticoat—one that I didn't have to make for myself, silly, isn't it?"

"Then you shall have it!" He lifted it from the rack where it hung. "It rustles beautifully—a good investment, I think!" and squeezed her hand, grinning. "Now we must find something for our youngest." They search around until on a peddlars stall they found a little wooden figure that swung on a trapeze when two wooden handles were squeezed together. The child loved it, fascinated by the little man turning somersaults and tumbling.

* * *

"It's been a wonderful day," said Mistress Meryatt as they drove home in the late afternoon. "One I shall never forget." The perfume of wild honeysuckle hung in the gentle breeze and lulled by the rocking of the cart the two children had fallen asleep, cradling their new toys in their arms, faces flushed from excitement and the fresh air. "Thank you, dear Walter, it's lovely having you home," and she leaned across and kissed him.

But lurking unspoken in the back of both their minds was the ever-present threat of Spain. How long could life like this continue?

CHAPTER 3

The Armada 1588

March had gone out like a lion and the wind, snapping dead branches from trees tossed rubbish along the High Street and over the quay into the harbour where it ebbed and flowed with the tides, echoing the mood of the inhabitants, for the trouble with Spain continued.

The Armada had been expected for months now, and the townspeople of Poole were complaining that trade was quiet—the Privy Council had placed an embargo on shipping to keep the mariners in port in readiness to fight, if the expected invasion came.

As a safeguard, Branksea Castle at the harbour's entrance was fortified with cannon and supplemented by smaller hand weapons, but this didn't help the beleaguered merchants.

The county had made preparations. A Muster Roll for Poole had been drawn up—giving detailed inventories of able-bodied men available to fight if and when the time arrived—and weapons, armour and horses listed for their use in time of battle. If the beacons were lit, Dorset's troops had orders to rendezvous with Somerset's at Dorchester and to follow the Armada along the coast from Poole to Portland, defending the coast against attack from the sea.

In addition, every man under the age of sixty had to have bows and arrows at the ready in his house, with practice at the butts taking place every Sunday and Holyday. They held competitions there, using the enforced task as sport and great was the rivalry amongst the young men of the town.

Steven and Ben's vessels were affected by the embargo and the two young men sat moodily on the quay steps picking at the faded paintwork of the lions and griffins of the coat of arms on the gun platform, listening to the slap, slap of waves against the hulls.

Steven stood up, brushing dried seaweed from his breeches and snapped a piece of driftwood, throwing it as far as he could out into the harbour.

"I hear that Poole has been asked to send a pinnace and a ship of sixty tons or more, to be ready by the end of the month—the Mayor of course pleads poverty saying it can't be done."

"I know, it makes me furious! We could go to Weymouth or Lyme, I s'pose," Ben's blue eyes were troubled. "They may not be so faint-hearted there."

"What do we live on—air? Do you know, I even tried the fishing boats yesterday—they said they had more than enough hands . . . Come on, let's get something to eat at the Three Mariners. The landlord may let us pay later, or work for it. He's expecting a windfall soon he told me, so p'raps he'll be feeling generous."

He pulled Ben to his feed and they made their way dispiritedly up the High Street until they reached the inn. John Berryman, landlord and Mayor was sitting in the settle by the fireside eating a pie. He greeted them warmly.

"Come and join me my good fellows. Will you take a noggin of ale and some food?"

"We would," said Steven hopefully, "but we can't pay for it!"

The landlord surveyed the pair sympathetically.

"Ah, times are hard for mariners—have this on me! These damned Spaniards, ruining trade!" He called for the pot-boy to bring some more pie and turned again to the cousins. "Well, and what are you two going to do this year?"

Steven pushed his curly hair away from his eyes, tilting back on the stool.

"We would LIKE to go to sea, or even be on standby to fight the Spaniards—but I understand Poole won't be furnishing a ship . . . what about *The Elephant*, she is lying idle?"

"Ah well," countered Berryman, warming to his favourite topic, "You see, the town has no money for such an undertaking! As you know, the pirates from Studland

Bay are continually robbing our poor ships." He gestured wildly. "We suffer losses of goods, losses of ships at sea . . . *The Elephant,* you say? Have you any idea of the cost of armaments nowadays . . .? Sails . . .?" He thumped the table, making his plate bounce and rattling his tankard. "You can't get them! Normandy canvas—the pirates grab it the moment the ships leave France. Something will have to be done—but not in MY mayoralty!"

The two young men exchanged glances. There wouldn't be any action here!

Steven rested his head on his hands, a faraway look in his grey eyes. "There're times I miss Lamorna," he mused. "With my own fishing boat I was beholden to no-one."

Ben glanced at him with concern. It wasn't often nowadays that he mentioned the past.

His cousin rubbed his short, neat beard pensively and stretched. "Still, those times are done and finished with. We've the future to think of now, whatever that'll bring. I sometimes think it's best we can't look ahead."

"Cheer up, Steve, this isn't like you! It's lack of food, I reckon!"

When the food was brought the two hungry young men set to with a will and conversation lapsed, the only sounds the clatter of plates from the kitchen, the whistling of the wind under the door and the crackling of logs in the fireplace. The landlord's dog crept nearer hoping for scraps, resting his warm chin on Stevens knee, brown eyes watchful for a crumb.

Suddenly the door burst open, letting a cold blast of air into the room and sending sparks flying up the chimney. A servant woman slid round the door and bobbed a curtsey.

"Master Berryman, Mistress Joan says will you be long? You are to dine with Master Greene today."

"Thank you Agnes." He dismissed her with a wave, saying to the cousins, "My father-in-law you know. Must keep in with him. Now HE'S a ship owner but he has other interests too. The thing is to DIVERSIFY. Don't put all your eggs in one basket. Mark my words and you'll do all right!"

Rising stiffly from the settle and brushing pie crumbs from his paunch he went towards the door.

"Well, I must leave you. Good luck!" and pulling his hat firmly on his head he went out into the windy street followed reluctantly by the dog, the door slamming behind them.

* * *

The month of May arrived. May Day was celebrated as usual with a maypole and dancing. 'Robin Hood and his Company' were present with archery contests, minstrels and players and there was music and feasting, but the enthusiasm of other years was missing. People couldn't relax—thoughts were with the Fleet under Lord Howard of Effingham, not on the jollifications so how could they concentrate on making merry?

The westerlies were roaring up the channel when, on the evening of Friday July 19th by the old calendar, the cousins were again strolling disconsolately on the quayside.

Ben's eyes had been ranging the distant horizon when suddenly he stopped, grabbed Steven by the arm and pointed to the Purbeck hills.

"What's that?"

"Hell's teeth—it's the BEACONS—LOOK!" shouted Steven, scanning the surrounding hills, and seeing others strung out along the coast like a chain of rubies. "The ARMADA'S on it's way!" The unthinkable had happened!

People hearing the commotion poked their heads from windows and began calling to others inside their houses, "The Armada, the Armada!" while women screeched to their children, "Come indoors or the Spaniards will get you!" Men poured from inns and taverns, gathering on the quayside pointing at the fires and buzzing with excitement—but making no move to put to sea.

Steven's face flushed with anger.

"This is abominable! Do we have to stand here helpless whilst our fellow mariners fight to the death out there . . .? Paugh!"

"Do you mean that?" said a quiet voice at his elbow.

"He turned. "Captain Trenchard! We would give our LIVES sir."

"Well, I'm giving my ship. She's small, but our fleet will need supplies, powder, ammunition, food and water. Are you fellows game to sail her?"

The cousins eyes shone with fervour. Action at last!

"Just give us a chance, sir!" cried Steven, speaking for both of them.

* * *

Inspired by Captain Trenchard, owners of small boats promised support. Men took their bows and arrows down from the racks, preparing to defend their homes and by the following Monday when the Armada was off the coast of Portland, little craft came streaming out of the creeks and ports of the county, bringing aid to the great fleet. With the inexplicable, unique spirit of comradeship that unites Englishmen of all walks of life in times of war, pirates from Studland under 'letters of marque', fishermen, yeomen and gentry joined with the Queen's Fleet against the common enemy.

The little ships from Dorset's ports went out to replenish the English vessels' supplies of gunpowder, food and water whilst on board Captain Trenchard's little ship Steven and Ben sailed close to the *Revenge.*

"Look," cried Ben, climbing the rigging, "there he is - Sir Francis Drake himself!" Steven followed the direction of his gesture and saw a stocky, copper haired man, face smeared by gunpowder who looked like the corsair he was.

"Good luck to you, Sir!" the cousins called and were rewarded with a wave.

Early next morning as the sun rose from the sea and the catspaws of wind ruffled the waves the two fleets jostled for position, each trying to outflank the other.

* * *

At Worth Master Bonville, seeing the beacons watched anxiously for the Armada, fearing a land attack, and when the great fleets appeared around the landmass of Portland he gave a shout.

Sarah had been feeding the chickens. Dropping the bucket she ran to the house, leaving the hens scrapping noisily over their unexpected bonus.

"What is it?"

"The damned Spanish are coming! Find your mistress and tell her I want her. Melchior must arm himself and prepare to do battle." He held his own bow in his hand which shook with a mixture of excitement and fear.

The rest of the household appeared, Mistress Bonville with flour on her apron which she pulled off, throwing it behind the settle.

Work was forgotten for once as they hurried down the rough path to the clifftop, the farm dog barking and snapping at their flying heels in excitement and Mistress Bonville puffing and blowing at the rear. People drifted in from all directions, seeking the best vantage points and gathered on the clifftops with their neighbours to watch the battle.

Melchior stood as near to Sarah as he could, trying to brush against her 'by accident' but she avoided him, managing to slip away by herself. She focused her attention on the fleet, attempting to recognize her beloved Poole ships—how she missed them! But they were too far away.

There was one huge Spanish vessel that caught the attention of the watchers on the clifftop though. She was the *Gran Griffon* and, as flagship to the slow supply ships, lagged behind the rest of the crescent until she was set upon by Francis Drake who sailed in close under her guns, blasting off a broadside.

"Come about!" he commanded joyously, eyes gleaming with the light of battle, sailing in under the *Gran Griffon's* stern and letting off another broadside. He followed through with musket fire, repeatedly risking his own neck to encourage his crew to greater acts of bravery. The Spanish vessel was badly damaged and her crew struggled to keep her afloat until at last she was towed back to the fleet by a galleass.

Back and forth raged the battle until Admiral Frobisher's fleet's repeated gunfire smashed the enemy, and at last they were compelled to abandon the action—but no invading Spaniard had landed on the Dorset coast!

* * *

Sarah, enjoying the unaccustomed freedom had spent it watching the battle, knowing everyone was too preoccupied to miss her. As the ships sailed away to the east she climbed over a drystone wall and passed through a little hollow. Rabbits startled by her presence slid away into the bushes and the breath of honeysuckle hung on the breeze. Carefully she picked her way up a bank and there before her was a splendid view of the coast in the magical, mystical evening light of Purbeck. Knowing she would be missed if she tarried any longer she sighed. The excitement was over and she would have to return to her dull routine. Had Steven been out there with the English fleet . . .? Praying into the wind so her words would be carried straight to God she breathed, Please let him survive these troubled times, and that night lay awake in her little bed, weaving fantasies to herself about his bravery in the battle.

* * *

The Armada was relentlessly pursued up the channel past the Isle of Wight, until at last at Dover the English trump card—the fireships—were brought in and bore down on the Spanish vessels, fire streaking out like horses' manes flying in the wind, leaving the Spanish ships burning, sinking and helpless.

Those vessels that survived, limping by the northern route back to Spain were ravaged by storms and gales and many more were wrecked on the rocky coats of Scotland and Ireland.

Queen Elizabeth, overjoyed at the success of her fleet commanded that Armada medals were to be struck, inscribed with the words, 'God breathed and they were scattered', distributing them to her gallant captains, while the people of England sighed with relief that—for the present—Spain had been defeated.

* * *

For the shipowners however, the embargo on shipping was still in force and those craft that were allowed to move from port to port did so under strict licence. This, of course did not deter pirates, who—their brief spell of loyalty forgotten—kept up their raids on British and foreign ships alike. Locally, their trade fell into the hands of a number of Purbeck men . . .

* * *

Melchior Strangeways trundled his cart stacked high with wine, fish and mutton along the Purbeck tracks. He had found for himself a nice, profitable trade in victualling the pirate ships and was rewarded with goods in exchange, which he then sold in the shops at Dorchester. Silks, satins and velvets from Italy were subjected to a high import duty, but using this 'back door' the pirates' goods were often on sale quite openly.

"Here y'are then!" he cried, halting on the seashore and the motley crew gathered around, haggling over his produce until the purser made him an offer for the lot.

"You can eat at the tavern, you dolts," the purser growled. "This is for when we put to sea again." His ship had arrived the previous evening, observed by workers in the fields of Purbeck who had passed the word on to their betters.

Master Bonville accompanied by Master Culliford of Encombe came riding down the track.

'Ah ha, and what have you brought us this time?" they called to the pirates, treating the event as a social occasion and fingering the rich silks and satins eagerly.

"Fine pickings, fine pickings for the gentlemen!" We've fur cloaks, fine velvets and jewellery for your ladies—and your wives!"

The landowners crossed to the tavern by the shore.

"We'll have a drink or two and a game of dice," called Bonville "and then select your wares."

Many a bargain could be had buying and selling pirate goods, and carts would creak through the heather tracks at the harbour's edge taking items to Wareham, Poole and farmsteads and houses throughout Purbeck.

This illicit trade had continued for some years, but it was too good to last . . .

CHAPTER 4

Francis Hawley

Frances Hawley was in a quandary. Sir Christopher Hatton, Vice Admiral of Purbeck had appointed him as his deputy. He enjoyed the position and was generally given a free hand in making decisions, but his present problem was his responsibility for the castle of Corfe.

Now from a distance all looked well, but the living quarters were in a pitiable state; Sir Christopher had decided he wanted them made habitable again and to the standards of a courtier, for was he not a favourite of the Queen herself and since 1587 Lord Chancellor of England? Indeed, she had granted him the castle for the princely sum of £4761 only a few years previously in 1572.

Hawley fingered his beard worriedly. Although he owned a moiety of the manor of Afflington and thirty four acres of sheep pasture at nearby Eastington he was building himself a house at Woodhouse near Studland, and had been using some of the materials and masons from the castle for his own purposes. He hadn't really MEANT to cheat the Vice Admiral but things had got out of hand. It was simply that the materials were there when he needed them. Workmen couldn't be trusted to deliver promptly and he wanted his house finished before winter set in. He had to find a way of getting more money before he was found out—and quickly!

Pushing his stool away from the table he paced the room in the Gloriette Tower of the castle, scowling, a frown furrowing his brow. Pausing at the window, hands clasped behind his back he studied the King's Tower across the courtyard. Sir Christopher even wanted the windows in the solid stone walls altered! They looked all right to him!

Returning to the table he took a gulp from the flagon of wine that was now half empty.

Steady, he told himself, this wouldn't help . . . or would it? He mused a while, toying with an idea that was forming. Wine, fine silks, velvets—there was a ready market for these amongst the gentlefolk. What was that he had heard in the inn the other day—talk bandied around by local landowners, Culliford, Uvedale, Bonville and the like of pirate captains bringing their goods ashore at Studland and selling them through the alehouses there? He was sure he had seen a decree somewhere amongst his papers saying that Queen Elizabeth and the Vice Admiral of Purbeck could have rights to pirate cargoes, or some such notion. Now, if he could get a cut of the profits—wouldn't that solve his problem?

Tossing the idea around for a while he felt rather pleased with himself, emptying the flagon with a grin and calling to a servant to saddle his horse. There was no time like the present, and time indeed was pressing!

He hurried to the muniment room and shuffled through the papers looking for the one he wanted. "Hmmm, Ralph Tresswell's surveys—must check on those sometime," briefly scanning a set of beautifully executed coloured maps of Purbeck and Corfe Castle which Sir Christopher had commissioned. "Ah, here it is," pouncing on a document, "This is the one I've been looking for."

Scanning it quickly he stuffed it into the pouch on his belt and ran down the staircase, pausing only to collect a cloak from his room and hurried along an ill-lit passage to the Martyr's Gate—believed to be the place where King Edward the Martyr was foully done to death—where his horse was ready saddled and waiting.

Clattering out across the drawbridge he swung to the left through the village, scattering chickens scratching in the roadway, and urging the animal to the top of the chalk ridge of East Hill and along the crest.

It was a fine day and his horse broke into an exhilarating gallop, fighting the bit and tossing his head in the wind, but Hawley was too occupied with his thoughts to admire the view of the black heathlands in the vale below where the red deer roamed, stretching to the harbours edge. A few miles further on to the east where Nine Barrow merged with Ballard Down, horse and rider slithered and slipped down the path towards Studland village. Using bit and spur he turned the beast aside from the route he usually took to his new house when travelling in this direction.

The horse side-stepped, convinced his master had chosen the wrong track but Hawley urged him forward through the trees and along the lane bordered by a small stream that trickled its way down to the sea. The animal laid its ears back, snorting at the noisy scene that confronted them as they turned the corner to William Munday's alehouse.

It was a low, single storey building with mouldering thatch coming away from the roof. Smoke blew from the chimney as he approached and he was reminded of the saying he had heard around Poole and Purbeck that 'Munday's house is the hell of the world and he the devil.'

Through the open door he saw a log blazing in the fireplace sending sparks flying up the wide chimney whilst all around were pirates, some singing bawdy songs and others brawling and fighting over the tavern women who were clad in gaudy cottons and grossgrains. Food and drink were spilt on the tables and the place smelt like a midden.

Now there were pirates like Francis Drake, who, prior to the Armada had completed his daredevil, reckless voyage around the world in the *Golden Hind*, returning laden with Spanish treasure to be knighted by the Queen and there was the other side of the coin, John Piers of Padstow.

The latter, a wench sitting on his lap, banged his tankard on the ale-slopped table calling for more beer. He was a tall, thin man with a black beard fuller at the ears than the chin, shoulder length hair and in spite of a life at sea, a sickly complexion. His once fine jacket stolen in a raid on a Dutch ship was stained and greasy, with damp sleeves where he had rested his arms on the slopped table top. Looking over his shoulder he spotted Hawley and, giving a roar toppled the woman from his lap on to the floor where she lay drunkenly giggling.

"What've we yer?" he bellowed, "A fine fellow come to join our band?"

Standing with hand on sword he answered stonily and with authority, "I am Francis Hawley, deputy Vice Admiral of Purbeck and as such it is my duty to board all ships in Studland bay to claim the rights of Queen Elizabeth and her Vice Admiral Sir Christopher Hatton, and this includes YOUR ship, Captain!"

Piers hauled himself to his feet, staggered and tripped over the woman on the floor. Shrieking with drunken laughter she grabbed him round the waist, showering him with kisses saying, "Let 'ee wait, John lad. You'll have more fun wi' me!"

Tossing her aside, the pirate captain furiously turned his attention to Hawley.

"What's this y'say—entitled to claim the rights of my cargoes for the Queen and your master? Do I hear 'ee right—and who's going to make me?" thundered Piers, a flush bringing colour to his pale cheeks.

"You hear me right," replied Hawley, a dangerous glint in his eye and standing his ground. "It is the law of the land and things could be very difficult for you unless you agree to accept my conditions . . . He paced up and down, turning abruptly, and looking craftily at the pirate captain, "However, I am a reasonable man and would not expect you to surrender EVERYTHING to her Majesty."

Unsure, Piers' eyes narrowed. He was not used to being confronted like this, and muttering he consulted with his cronies.

Seeing his advantage, Hawley pressed home.

"My man George Fox will be along later and together we will inspect the goods you have stored in the large barn by the church."

Pleased with the way things appeared to be going he was amazed at his own courage—born of desperation. Inclining his head in a terse nod to Piers he turned on his heel and walked on air back to his mount. The plan was working!

Once out of sight of the tavern, he rode quickly to Woodhouse where his new house built of ironstone from the nearby quarry was almost completed, the only sign of activity a thatcher stacking his unused straw in a corner ready to take it away.

George Fox opened the door and came to meet him. He was Hawley's officer and lived there temporarily with his own servant John Baker, a rough, wizened man who supplemented his living by fishing and was well acquainted with the pirates from nearby Studland and if the truth were known, not averse to doing the odd deal with them himself.

"Well, what do you think of it?" called Fox. "It will be completed this week."

"I've not come to talk about the house," said Hawley, swinging his leg over the horse's back, sliding to the ground and brushing the dust from his clothes. Putting his arm around Fox's shoulders he led him away from the workman. "I've a plan . . ."

When he was done, Fox looked at him thoughtfully. "IS this legal? he queried.

"Well, I did hear something like it was being practised elsewhere in the west country and I've got this decree—here, you have a look at it . . . but the thing that matters is, PIERS believes it to be true so we should be on safe ground."

"But he is a dangerous man—he'd think nothing of killing us!"

"Not if he thinks the forces of law and order can be summoned by Sir Christopher. Don't forget, I could get the pirate captains hung or at least imprisoned on the authority of the Vice Admiral of Purbeck."

Fox considered, scanning the paper. If they had Hatton's word to back them up they should be on safe ground. "Oh very well. On your head be it!" he said wearily. "I'll get my horse and we'll see what we can achieve."

When they reached the great barn, Piers was waiting along with two other pirate chiefs—Clinton Atkinson, a tall well-educated man with a long pale face and thin whiskers and John Newman from nearby Poole—stocky, middle aged and a deceptively honest face, an unlikely pair of pirates, and some of their crewmembers.

Piers glowered at the deputy Vice Admiral and together

the pirates reluctantly opened the heavy doors, displaying an Aladdin's cave of goods—spices, raisins, sugar, hats decorated with fine plumes, timber of the best quality, wine and brandy. Incongruously a pile of bibles lay in a corner with packs of playing cards whilst stacked in bales on the other side were velvets, satins, silks and a silver mirror, with more goods at the rear of the barn.

"Gather round," called Hawley. "Can you all hear me?" They shuffled their feet and mumbled their assent. "Now this is what I propose to do," he told the assembled pirates. "You give me first choice,and I will arrange for you to sell your goods in the Isle of Purbeck without hindrance." The captains looked at each other warily. This didn't seem so bad!

Hawley decided to begin on a small scale and increase his share gradually. Making a list of goods to be delivered to the castle of Corfe, in his atrocious handwriting he wrote:

2 sugar loaves
12 lbs of ginger
a fair pair of hand irons and tongs
half a dozen fine stools
a silk cushion
1 silver mirror
and a fine little waggon to carry the goods in.

"Mark well," he repeated addressing the pirates, "from now on, my man John Baker will inform me of the arrival of your ships, whereupon he will row me out to your vessels and I will take first choice. When I have chosen—on behalf of our Gracious Queen and Sir Christopher Hatton of course—the rest of the goods will be free to sell in Purbeck—understood?"

"Aye," they muttered, still not quite sure if this was legal or not. Never mind, there was plenty more where this came from!

"Right, we'll be on our way and we will see you again soon."

Hawley and Fox wheeled their horses and riding back together were highly satisfied at the outcome. They had saved face and the wrath of Sir Christopher and would also do very nicely with a profit on the side as time went by, and Hawley's house was saved.

* * *

The changing seasons passed and work went on apace at the castle. Surprisingly the pirates found Hawley's scheme suited them very well as they now had a ready market for their goods and there was little danger to themselves, having as they had the blessing of the Vice Admiral of Purbeck on their ventures.

Francis Hawley surveyed the scene contentedly. Well, it's coming along nicely, he thought to himself. The castle stood high on its small hill in the gap of the Purbeck range, with an outer 'curtain' wall surrounding it. The building work entailed the lowering of ceilings and putting in extra rooms.

He wandered across to the Kings tower where there was still scaffolding. Masons had toiled on the stonework and marble for months and he was pleased to see the newly altered windows were almost finished. A fine external gallery of three round arches spanned the tower with two storeys of small square rooms, while across from that section was the neat and elegant, newer Gloriette Tower with the best apartments for noblemen and women of the castle.

Panelling work had still to be carried out—Sir Christopher had ordered medallions in the latest style, with linen fold panels on some new coffers for his own apartments. New heavily carved armchairs were being made for the Long Hall and everywhere the fragrant smell of planed timber hung in the air. Some windows were covered with oiled cloth to keep out the weather while others were glazed, and in these rooms rich tapestry hung around the walls and across the doorways.

He felt he had done a good job. Sir Christopher had said that he wanted the work completed by Christmas. That gave him three more months—yes, he had achieved much since his appointment!

From the corner of his eye he caught sight of a

horseman, hurrying along in a cloud of dust on the road from Wareham. Immediately alert he thought, "Who could this be?" He didn't recognise him.

The man reigned in his mount at the castle gate and presented his credentials. They were obviously in order as he was admitted. Dismounting, he watched his horse being led away to the stables in the outer bailey, whilst brushing the dust from his clothes.

Presently Hawley heard a knock on his door and a servant entered.

"A message from Sir Christopher Hatton, Master Hawley."

"Give it here then, fool."

"The messenger wishes to deliver it into your own hands, Master."

"He has obviously heard you are a nincompoop." The servant glowered. "Very well—very well, give it here,"he went on, agitatedly, wondering what this meant. Sir Christopher had left him very much to his own devices regarding matters in Purbeck whilst he spent most of his time at Court with Queen Elizabeth or at his estate, Holdenby Palace in Northampton.

Bowing, the messenger handed over the paper. Breaking the seal Hawley scanned it hastily.

"Sir Christopher . . . coming for Christmas with guests . . . prepare festivities and entertainments . . . engage servants . . . Hell's Teeth!" he muttered, this was a massive task and the building work not yet completed! He had been about to ride over to Aflington to see his favourite falcon and to get some fresh air but that would have to go by the board now . . . Then, remembering the laws of hospitality and wishing to give a good impression to his master's messenger he called the servant and bid him feed and house the man for the night.

That done, his thoughts turned again to the shattering news. He picked up a quill to make a list but the point was thick, so cursing he re-fashioned it with his pen knife. Already he could feel a headache coming on.

"There will be dancing of course. A tournament—that is always popular and can take place in the outer bailey. Now let's see, we need sixty paces in length and forty in width running east to west with a gate at each end for the Lists. A Royal Box for the guests. A masque—oh Gods Wounds, how will I ever get this organised?"

This would be the first event of importance to be held at the castle since it came into Sir Christopher's hands and poor Hawley was at his wits end. There were others living in the castle besides him but they were only impoverished gentry.

"They must all lend a hand, that's it," he concluded deciding to appeal to them at the meal in the Great Hall that evening. Folding the paper he put it into his wallet and decided to lie down for a while. It had been a very trying day!

* * *

Hawley's man, George Fox rode along the cliff-top at Ballard Down watching William Vaughan's *Mayflowyre* sailing like a cloud by Handfast Point and into the bay. From where he sat he could hear screeching, jabbering and laughter coming from her decks, and curious to discover the source, turned his horse down Water Lane towards Munday's tavern. As he watched, a boat was lowered and rowed ashore.

Vaughan hailed him across the sheltered water. "Are you coming aboard? You'll see we have a goodly haul!"

Fox acknowledged him. "Yes, row me out, will you?"

The keel of the rowing boat scraped on the sand and Fox climbed aboard, seating himself amid-ships.

"What was all that noise?" he asked one of the oarsman. They had become friendly over the months Hawley had been dealing with the pirates, in fact many of the local Purbeck gentry had found some—but not all—of the pirate captains to be exceedingly good company.

"Ha ha—'twas monkeys and parrots! Would you believe, some of they birds talk's good as you or me! And they monkeys! Like funny liddle people they be, always up to tricks. But don't they jabber!"

They reached the *Mayflowyre* and Fox climbed aboard, puffing and blowing from the steep ascent.

"Ah, Fox," said Vaughan. "Wait till you see what we have this time."

There on view were eleven trunks, open, their contents spread over the deck. Strutting around was the mate wearing a violet cloak over a crimson satin doublet decorated with silver lace, brightly coloured stockings and a velvet hat, making exaggerated bows to the monkeys, while the crew fell about with laughter.

Vaughan himself was wearing a cloak of tawny brown over his seagoing clothes.

"Where did these come from?" asked Fox, looking in amazement at the beautiful quality of the clothes heaped on the deck and fingering the softness of the materials in his hands.

Vaughan sniggered. "Shall we say that the English Ambassador in Scotland will soon be looking a little shabby!" and laughed his braying laugh."

"You DIDN'T!"

Receiving no denials, Fox had to accept that he did!

"Well, what shall I take for Hawley?"

"Take him that gilt rapier . . . and that bible! There's a tailor in Corfe that I've promised a cloak to. I'll sell him that puce valance, I'm not partial to the colour myself. Clinton Atkinson wants a black cloak . . . that one over there with the lace looks his style." He laughed again. "The crimson silk stockings are for the Mayor of Poole and the other bible's for Parson Cook of Sandwyche. Well distributed, don't you think?"

* * *

Piracy had become more and more acceptable as a way of life, especially when a cheap bargain could be had, and many was the eye in high places that was blindly turned to their dealings . . .

But some people objected. Things began to get out of hand, so to cover himself Hawley wrote to the Privy Council:

"My duty is to drive these pirates hence. I cannot cope, I have no backing from the landowners, the pirates are strong and cannot be repulsed . . . but my conscience is clear—however, I have no money for munitions, so there is little I can do . . ." and continued with his pirates' trade.

CHAPTER 5
Steven Curnow

Steven Curnow, although he didn't realise it yet had come to a cross roads in his life. Despite earlier misgivings he HAD survived the last couple of years he mused, gazing into his tankard of ale in the 'Three Mariners'. There had been several profitable voyages with Meryatt and the *Bountifull Gyfte* before the shipping embargo, then the replenishing of the Fleet at the time of the Armada—a far cry from his boyhood fishing days in Cornwall . . . but enough of the past, he must FORGET . . .

"And now what?" he thought, emptying his tankard. The trouble with Spain was unresolved and the embargo on the movement of shipping between ports remained in force. This was still hampering trade and Meryatt was finding it more and more difficult to find cargoes. Should he act on what Berryman had advised before the Armada—to diversify? But if he did, in which direction?

A skinny dog skulked into the inn sniffing around the rushes looking for scraps, until the innkeeper's shout sent it scurrying through the door where it collided with two customers coming in. One of them sent it on its way with a kick whilst the other looked about for an empty table, and finding none, asked Steven if they could share his.

"Of course, sirs. It doesn't do a man good to drink alone. Landlord, drinks for these gentlemen."

"Most civil," said the older of the two. He was dressed in brown velvet doublet and matching hose with a white ruff around his neck—undoubtedly a person of high standing. "May I introduce myself? I am Francis Hawley of Corfe Castle and this is my officer, George Fox."

"Steven Curnow, late of Cornwall, the past three years with the *Bountifull Gyfte*—and tomorrow—who knows?"

replied Steven, his brow furrowed in a wry grin and extending his hand.

Hawley glanced sideways at Fox. "Who knows indeed? Do I take it you are seeking a change?"

Steven explained his position, rocking back on his stool and waiting with curiosity to see what Hawley was about to propose.

"I am opening up Corfe Castle for Christmas for Sir Christopher Hatton's visit. There is much work to be done and I need workmen and servants for several weeks plus musicians for the Yuletide festivities. Are you interested?"

Steven pondered for a moment. It would certainly be a change and a prospect of a Christmas at Corfe Castle might be a diversion. His teeth showed in a sudden smile, lighting up his face.

"Yes, why not?" he replied. "By that time the problems at sea may have resolved themselves. When do you want me?"

"Right away," said Hawley, scratching his chin through his pointed beard. "Present yourself tomorrow morning at the castle. Where are you staying? Fox, write a pass for him to hand in at the gate and have it delivered today without fail."

Finishing their drinks the two men ordered another but Steven bade them farewell until tomorrow, leaving in search of Master Meryatt. Although his ship was apparently in dock for the foreseeable future it was only fair to break the news personally, and he had to find his cousin Ben. Perhaps he could also be persuaded to join him and he too might welcome the prospect of a Christmas at Corfe?

Walking with a spring in his step that had been missing for some time he went along the narrow High Street where the gabled houses leaned towards each other. Avoiding the rubbish and piles of timber blocking the footpath he passed the old woman's house and remembered the young Sarah. I wonder how she is faring in Purbeck? he thought idly then noticed a familiar figure in shirt, leather breeches and jerkin with long sea boots coming out of an alehouse, and immediately forgot her.

"Ben, lad," he called. "I've a proposition for you."

His cousin, a cheerful young man with merry blue eyes always looking for adventure was dark haired like Steven and he too sported a short neat beard which made him look like a corsair. Although half a head shorter, he was much the same build as his cousin with the strong, muscular chest and biceps of a mariner.

"Too late," he smiled, "I've just got myself a passage to the New Found Land."

"At this time of the year?" Steven's face darkened. "Only fools sail in the autumn—there're storms and icebergs, you young idiot! And what about the embargo?"

"That's no problem, the master's got a permit from the Vice Admiral of Purbeck and we sail late in the season to bring back those that've been fishing out there all summer. It's good money, ten shillings a month and it's on the *Prymrose.* I've always liked her, as y'know."

Steven recalled the vessel. She was a ship of about one hundred and twenty tons, seams well caulked and sails neatly stowed—a trim craft, he had to admit but it still seemed a foolhardy voyage at this end of the year. It was hard enough in the spring!

"Well, good luck to you lad, but you could have had an easier berth at Corfe Castle. I'm to be there for some weeks, preparing the place for Christmas for that same Vice Admiral." He put his hand on Ben's shoulder." Come on boy, change your mind!" but even as he said it he saw the stubborn look in his cousin's blue eyes and knew he would be aboard the *Prymrose* when she sailed.

"I'm a mariner, not a landsman, and that's a fact that'll never change," said Ben, shaking his head. "What's more I've signed on and it's agreed that we sail on the morning tide. I'll not go back on my word."

Two revellers came out of the alehouse and the cousins stepped aside to let them go on their way, singing and weaving down the street, arms supporting each other towards the quay.

Steven realised this was the parting of the ways. Huskily, he said "Well then, God speed Ben, if you won't be persuaded . . . I trust you'll have a safe journey and I'll see you when you return."

Embracing, the two young men hugged each other tightly. They had no other relatives and they had always been as close as brothers.

Steven turned away, a lump in his throat. The sea could be a cruel mistress . . .

* * *

The following morning dawned sunny. He set out very early, avoiding the departure of the *Prymrose* and his spirits lifted on the ride across the heath. The river banks at Wareham were boggy and he negotiated them carefully, not wanting to arrive covered in mud. As he rode through the sparse forest, deer startled by his passing scattered away into the silver birches, the dappled sunshine camouflaging their presence. Birds sang out, breathing the clear fresh air at last he felt it was good to be alive!

Presenting himself and his pass at Corfe Castle he was shown the inner and outer baileys, the stables, the defensive towers in the curtain walls and lastly the King's Tower, Gloriette and kitchens of the inner ward.

He was to start work at once and the steward gave him his allotted tasks. To begin with he was to assist the carpenter with panelling, but on board ship he had been able to turn his hand to anything and he enjoyed the work. He was handy with plane and saw and each day was filled with the smell of freshly cut seasoned timber. The food was good, too. Autumn was the season of plenty when beasts for which there was insufficient fodder to over-winter were slaughtered and eaten. There was fruit in abundance in the orchards and fresh bread from the kitchens.

At last the building alterations were almost completed. Hawley had supervised the work himself and was pleased with Steven who had worked hard and willingly and was scrupulously honest.

One day he summoned him to his presence.

"I have a job for you my boy. I want you to ride out to the neighbouring farms and check on the availability of food for the festivities. I'll give you a list of the items we are looking for. You can place orders but get the best prices you can. My lord is not made of money, you know."

He was relieved to be out in the open air again and breathed deeply, smelling rain in the wind and the tang of the distant sea. Not used to spending so much time indoors he relished the thought of the comparative freedom this latest task would bring. In a contented frame of mind he spent the next few days riding around and familiarising himself with the Purbeck countryside.

Riding along the crest of Emmetts Hill, a high promontory near St. Aldhelm's Head he came across a small farmstead nestling in a sheltered valley. The outlook was superb—in the foreground the conical shape of Hounstout and stretching away to the west the grey cliffs of Kimbridge culminating in the turreted face of Gad Cliff, rising almost five hundred feet sheer from the sea.

The house itself was small, built of local stone with a couple of outbuildings and reminded him with a pang of his home in Lamorna. He could visualise this place at the time of harvest with the fields swaying heavy-eared with wheat, oats and barley. There were a few cattle for milk and beef grazing nearby, a couple of house-pigs grunted from their sty with chickens scratching about the yard. If ever I give up the sea, he thought this is the kind of place where I could settle.

He rode down the track from the sheltering hill and drew rein at the door of the farmhouse. An old man, hearing the horse came out, bent and slow.

"Greetings, maaster," he called in a quavery voice, pulling of his cap. "What can I do for 'ee?"

"I'm buying up goods for Sir Christopher Hatton at Corfe Castle. He only wants the best, but I can see your fowls look plump and well cared for. Do you have any you can spare?"

"Aar, I'll be selling 'em anyhow. I'll not stay yer through the winter. Come you in, come you in, good maaster and take a sup of ale," and he beckoned him into the house.

Steven followed him into the stone-flagged kitchen. The old fellow had kept it as neat as he could but it lacked a woman's touch.

"My missus died last winter, and 'tis all I can do to keep a-goin'. So I be movin' to Wareham to me dorters. Sir Christopher's man, that Maaster 'Awley says I'm to stay on yer till 'e gets a new tenant, but 'tis all I can do. Can't keep 'un clean as a daisy no more, crippled with this ache in me old bones and only a boy to help 'un. Still, I do reckon t'wont be long afor I joins me missus an' I shan't be sorry. 'Tidn't the same without 'un," and his eyes grew watery.

Steven patted the old fellow consolingly on the shoulder.

"I'll speak to Master Hawley and ask him to hurry and find a new tenant. You'll have a good few years yet in comfort with your daughter, and Wareham is a fine town."

"We'll see, we'll see, said the old man, "and thank 'ee, young 'un."

Steven rode thoughtfully back along the track. HE wasn't ready for life ashore yet, but he would ask around and try to find a tenant for the place. He had liked the old fellow and wanted to help him if he could.

* * *

It is strange how life turns out, he mused. He was on a hill which extended around three sides of a valley with the sea on the fourth side. He had heard it called the golden bowl of Encombe, where gentry lived and he could understand why. It was a far cry from his native Cornwall but he loved it here.

He was resting his horse, lying under a tree and watching the clouds sail majestically overhead for all the world like heavenly barques, his whole being absorbing the tranquillity of the scene spread before him. The sweet smell of grass, woodbine on a bush and the only sounds the trilling of larks high above and the gentle soughing of the breeze through the gorse, and for a moment, high on the hill he felt like a god.

Suddenly his horse raised its head, whickering softly.

Someone coming, he thought, sitting up and shielding his eyes, peering into the slanting afternoon sun at a figure that came towards him carrying a basket.

He was subconsciously admiring the silhouette through

half-closed eyes against the light as the figure approached when there was a gasp, then a chuckle.

"Why—Steven Curnow as I live and breathe!" The lithe, female figure came around the tree, placing the empty basket on the ground beside him.

Puzzled, he looked at her questioningly and in the pause a yaffingale chuckled from a nearby wood. Scrambling to his feet and turning his back to the sun he saw the unforgettable tawny/green eyes of the girl Sarah in this lovely young woman, and the yaffingale chuckled again.

He stared at her speechlessly feeling his heart trip, until she too laughed her familiar laugh.

"Oh Steven, you look like a moonstruck calf. I surely haven't changed that much, or have you forgotten me? On the quay at Poole . . .? haunting the ships . . .?" she prompted, smiling.

Recovering, he laughed too.

"You certainly HAVE changed, little Sarah and decidedly not for the worse!"

"Well, I feel just the same," she said warmly.

"How have you been? I've often wondered how you were faring. Have you found any of your adventures?"

"Did you really think about me?" She came and sat beside him under the tree. "I suppose I like it well enough here, but except for the Armada it has been so DULL and no-one laughs—they're all solemn and work so hard. There is one awful fellow called Melchior Strangeways," she laughed at his expression. "Yes, that really is his name—and I have to keep avoiding him. He works for Master Bonville but I'm sure he's in league with the pirates . . . Oh, Steven, it IS good to see you, but whatever are you doing HERE, so far from the *Bountifull Gyfte*?"

He was bringing her up to date with the embargo on shipping and an account of his life at the castle when she suddenly sprang to her feet.

"Oh goodness, I'm sorry—I'm late—they will wonder what I've been up to! I was delivering pies to the vicar of St. James's at Kingston. Mistress Bonville makes and sells them, and she'll say I have been dallying and dreaming again."

"Oh Sarah, you are right, you haven't changed, have you?" laughed Steven. Except in appearance, he thought. Why, she was beautiful now. Who would have thought the boyish figure could be transformed into this lovely young woman! Hurriedly he tried to think of a way to detain her, then had an inspiration.

"We can get there faster on horseback," he said quickly. "Melody is rested now and I will take you as far as the farm if you show me the way."

"Oh lovely, thank you kind sir," she made an exaggerated curtsey and smiled, her cheeks flushing with pleasure as he swung her up in front of him, saying he would hold her round the waist—for safety's sake.

They cantered along the hilltop, her hair blowing back tickling his nose, laughing together all the way until they were almost at the farm.

"You'd better leave me at the end of the track, Master Bonville is very strict about my comings and goings," she said as she dismounted.

Holding her hand before she could slip away, he said quietly "And when do you come this way again?"

"Every Thursday," her eyes dancing.

"Until next Thursday then?"

"Of course!" Life could be good after all, and giving him a smile and a wave, she ran down the track to the farm, fair curls bouncing. Her look smote straight into his soul and he felt the earth lurch, arousing feelings he thought were over, realising his world would never be quite the same again . . .

* * *

Behind the stone barn a man lurked. The bane of Sarah's life, Melchior Strangeways had attempted to waylay her on more than one occasion, once even managing to corner her in the hen house only to have himself spattered with eggs when he tried to kiss her.

Never having forgiven her for being rejected at their first meeting and, seeing her slide down from the horse of this personable young man, his blood boiled and he muttered "I'll get you, Miss Hoity-Toity, you see if I don't!"

* * *

The following Thursday was uncompromisingly wet but Steven, nothing daunted, with a heavy cloak slung round his shoulders rode to the farm in the morning not knowing what time Sarah would set out, keeping watch from the cross roads and sheltering under a hawthorn tree.

Strangeways was crossing the yard when he recognised him by his horse.

"Ah, so that's the way things be," he thought and waited his opportunity.

Steven caught sight of Sarah as she went to the byre to collect the eggs. Tying Melody's reins to the tree he slipped around the back of the building and gave a low whistle. Her face lit up when she heard him and as the rain was falling heavily, beckoned him inside.

"Got you!" muttered Strangeways and, seizing his opportunity ran to the farmhouse.

"Master, master, there be people a-talking in the byre. I think it be beggars!" he called. Now if there was one thing that Richard Bonville detested it was a vagabond.

"Oh there are, are there? We will see about that!" he growled, picking up a thick stick from a corner by the fire and heading out into the rain.

His wife called from the kitchen, "Wait for me," pushing back her stool and throwing a shawl around her shoulders against the rain. Farm life could be dull and she didn't want to miss any excitement!

Hurrying across the muddy yard they reached the byre intent on trouble. Flinging open the door of the shed Master Bonville saw the pair together.

"What's this—who is this man?" he cried, brandishing his stick at Steven.

Mistress Bonville pushed past him, and saw Sarah.

"Wanton!" she screamed, spittle flying from her mouth in her rage. "Leave this place at once with your fornicator and never let me see you again, you ungrateful hussy!"

Sarah, white with shock was at a loss for words.

"You are mistaken!" Steven thundered. "This girl is blameless. I have known . . ." but Bonville wouldn't let him finish.

"I have the evidence of my own eyes. There is only one reason for a man to meet a girl secretly in a byre. Get out—the pair of you and never show your faces here again!"

"Oh, we will go all right! You have never shown me any affection and I should have earned much more than my food and bed, but I have not a penny to show for it. Come, Steven! and she turned on her heel, perfectly in command of herself, green eyes flashing with anger.

"You do the girl a grave injustice, sir!" said Steven angrily and followed her from the byre to his horse, putting his cloak about her shoulders protectively and helping her to mount.

"Don't you want to collect any of your things from the house?" he asked before they rode away.

"And have them accuse me of stealing? No thanks! Oh dear, Steven—this is a pretty pass," then she giggled, looking very like the child of two years ago. "What will become of me?"

He smiled ruefully, giving her an impulsive hug.

"This is all my fault—I will take care of you. We'll go to Corfe. I know Master Hawley is still looking for help at the castle, so that will take care of the immediate future, anyhow . . . Don't fret, Sarah."

"Do I look as though I'm fretting?" she replied impishly as they left the farm and rode along the narrow lane, Steven's cloak scattering the raindrops from the hedgerow.

"I believe you're enjoying yourself" he countered. "Look, the sky is clearing. It'll be sunny before long," and even as he spoke a finger of light pointed from the clouds towards the castle of Corfe.

"It is an omen. Life is about to improve like the weather," and she smiled up at him contentedly, her face lighting up like the sunshine.

"You funny little soul. Your world has been turned upside-down and you are smiling!" he said tenderly as, Sarah sitting in front, they rode off along the crest of the chalk downland together.

Making their way along the track he drew her attention to the drops of water that clung to the hedgerows reflecting the sunlight, sparkling like diamonds, and contentedly they breathed the musty, autumnal scent of dead leaves that hung heavily in the air.

"Really," she said after a few minutes, "considering I have thrown myself on your mercy I know very little about you, save that you were a seaman on the *Bountifull Gyfte.* From your voice I'd guess that you're not originally from these parts?"

Shaking his head he said, "I came from Cornwall where my parents had a farm and I a fishing boat." A strange, guarded expression came over his face and he went quiet.

Searching for something to make him smile again she said, "Lamorna—what a pretty name."

"It means 'Valley by the sea' in the Cornish tongue," he explained pensively, his thoughts still far away, leaving her wondering what had happened there to change his mood, but sensitive enough not to ask.

They rode on towards Corfe where the hills loomed up out of the mist like islands in the ocean, and the castle seemed to float in the clouds giving the landscape a strange, ethereal appearance.

Sarah, relaxed and at ease now, began humming the tune that had been on her lips that last morning in Poole, so long ago it seemed another lifetime.

He looked down at her from hooded eyelids.

"You've a sweet voice, 'My Lady Greensleeves', he muttered huskily. "That description fits you well."

Not meeting his gaze, she sang the words softly.

"Alas, my love you do me wrong . . ."

Steadily he looked at her. She was so vulnerable, sitting there in front of him in that ridiculous green dress, moulded to her body by the rain. There were things he wanted to say to her but this was neither the time nor the place.

Pulling himself together he said, "There, just across the common and over the hill and we will be at the village. Are you ready for another new beginning?"

CHAPTER 6

Ben Curnow

"Well, there aren't too many men fool enough to risk their necks on such a voyage, especially this late in the season," admitted the master of the *Prymrose*, honestly. His double chin spilled over the neck of the shirt that he wore with sleeves rolled above his brawny forearms, while a worn tunic covered his portly figure. He was wearing knee breeches held up by a belt with an unusual shining copper buckle,and on his legs were long sea boots. Bright eyes twinkled merrily out of his chubby face as he greeted the new arrival.

"I probably AM a fool but my neck is my own, so the risk is mine, too," said Ben with an answering grin.

The master liked him at once, hoping this lad would survive the arduous journey and return safely. He slapped him on the back saying, "Welcome aboard, lad!"

Ben stowed his gear in the crew's quarters and was making himself familiar with the ship when a few minutes later he heard murmuring voices on the quay alongside. Swinging up the ladder to come back on deck he shielded his eyes from the sun, and looking about him noticed some of the other crew members bidding farewell to their loved ones.

It was to be a hazardous voyage and the fear of possible failure was suddenly brought home to him. His face lost its grin as he watched a young, obviously pregnant woman dressed in a patched gown with a shawl over her head, weeping, holding the grubby hand of a wide-eyed urchin and unwilling to let go of her husband. He was a young fellow in a tarred canvas jacket and woollen cap, with red curly hair and eyes the colour of the ocean, trying not to look relieved at the prospect of being at sea again and away from the ties of his little family. Catching Ben's eye he winked at him over his wife's shoulder.

Looking away, not wanting to intrude Ben saw another, older man with grizzled grey hair and beard quietly embracing a middle aged woman whose face was stiff with the effort of being brave at the parting. She had been through this many times before and knew what it was like to wait for a ship long overdue. Pulling reluctantly away her husband ran up the gangplank, turning once to give a final salute.

Ben hated farewells and was glad he and Steven had said theirs the night before. He shivered as though someone had walked over his grave as a sudden breeze caught some rubbish lying on the quay, swirling it up into the air in a miniature whirlwind.

"It's good to see we 'ave one more seaman aboard to make up the number," called another of the mariners cheerfully, beckoning him over. "Goin' ter make yer fortune wi' us then?"

Ben gave himself a mental shake and grinned, his cheerful nature reasserting itself.

The rest of the crew seeing him standing near the mainmast shouted a greeting—they were a friendly bunch and he knew a couple of them by sight. Warming to their friendly exuberance he joined them and they chatted and joked for a while, talking of tides, weather lore and women until a shout from the master reminded them of their duties.

"Come on, me hearties, the tide be right so cast off the moorings and hoist the bow sprit sail."

They swung into action smoothly, the land forgotten, restored to their rightful element—the sea.

The *Prymrose* gracefully gained momentum and steerage as she answered the rudder, seemingly eager to put to sea again. The master called out commands and the voyage was under way, the crew's muscles standing out like cords on their arms and shoulders as they hauled aloft the high peaked lateen sail which instantly caught the breeze and filled.

Ben soon swung into the familiar pattern of setting sail.

Little waves slapped merrily against the bow of the ship as she skirted the long, tawny island of Branksea, weaving her way along the deep water channel. Although the harbour was wide, it was very shallow for the most part and many a craft had come to grief by going aground on the mud flats where the waders fished and cormorants arranged themselves in rows.

Reaching the harbour mouth the master called for the square mainsail to be hoisted. Rhythmically the men hauled it into position. The sail slatted and filled and the *Prymrose* was a fine sight heading past Studland bay, around the chalk stacks of Handfast Point and westwards into the Channel.

For the rest of the day they slowly made their way into the wind, past the village of Sandwyche in its sandy bay and along the rugged limestone coast of Dorset. Stoneworkers labouring in the quarries paused from hewing the heavy blocks, giving them a wave as they passed. On St. Aldhelm's Head the ancient little chapel could be seen standing out against the skyline.

Ben glanced warily upwards, not liking what he saw—the weather had changed since their departure. Creamy cumulo-nimbus clouds moved imperceptibly up from the horizon slowly filling the arc of the sky. The light turned purple and crimson, reflecting the sun's strange glow from the towering clouds making them appear almost solid, like mountains and caverns. His troubled eyes watched as heavy, anvil shaped storm clouds reared above their fellows and the speed of the wind increased. The little *Prymrose*, dwarfed by the enormity of the sea fought her way bravely through the troughs of the rising waves.

The sea was growing perceptibly rougher, and as the first night of their long journey fell his fears were justified. The wind was dead ahead and they were hardly making any headway.

"Curse this damned wind!" exclaimed the master. "We shall have to beat before it."

Using the rudder and sprit sail the crew moved the ship's head away from the wind increasing her forward speed, but in a tacking zig-zag motion.

"Helm to starboard!" cried the master, attempting to swing the bows across the eye of the wind, and the men hastily reset the yards and sails for the new course.

In spite of their efforts, although the *Prymrose* was sailing a fair distance she wasn't making much forward progress, merely struggling to and fro on a broad reach. This was very time-consuming and the night was getting wilder and darker.

The wind was worsening and the master's normally cheerful face bore a worried frown as the little ship neared the Portland race, graveyard of many a proud vessel.

On the coast the wind was reaching hurricane force. Branches torn from trees flew in the air like uncanny birds of prey. Trees themselves were uprooted and people cowered indoors, hiding from the might of the storm. Stock sheltered as best they could behind drystone walls and birds were dashed from their refuges, smashing into the ground, their small corpses lying sodden where they fell.

The master called encouragement to his crew whilst the wind whistled in the rigging and spray torn from the crest of the billows rattled on the deck.

"Reef in the sails!" he cried and all hands swiftly climbed aloft in the bucking shrouds to do his bidding.

The ship was sliding backwards down the waves as they overtook her, when suddenly out of a squall the hurricane hit them with terrible force tearing the mainsail stays from their frozen hands before it was properly stowed, splitting it down the middle.

Hail stung their exposed flesh making them colder than ever. The ship wallowed in a trough, her crew hanging on for grim death when a mighty wave struck the vessel, snatching the tiller from the master's hands and knocking him aside.

The *Prymrose* came about, starboard beam into the wind. Another huge wave crashed into her followed immediately by a great gust of wind which roared up from the west. Everywhere was noise and movement then with a terrible rending and groaning the mainmast snapped like a stick. Rigging fell in a confused tangle making movement even more difficult on the slanting decks.

Before Ben's eyes the red-headed lad was caught by a wave knocking him off his feet. The master's warning shout was lost in the gale as the lad was swept overboard and to their horror swirled away to his death. There was no question of going back for him, the *Prymrose* was out of control now.

They could see the grizzled-haired man was also in difficulties, caught in the rigging and hanging over the side. Ben struggled to reach him, stretching out his arm as far as he could, almost losing his balance. Their eyes met desperately. "Hold on!" he yelled but was repeatedly driven back by the sea, gasping, drenched by waves breaking over the ship. Battling his way to the side again he saw the man's grip loosen in the icy water and he too was washed away, sinking below the waves and disappearing.

They were in real difficulties now, but worse was to come. Heeling over, all planks creaking and protesting the ship came broadside on to the heavy seas with Ben clinging to a rail, when without warning a spar swung loose and caught him a crashing blow to the head. The world seemed to whirl about him in a storm of noise, lightning and blackness and he slumped unconscious to the deck . . .

In the darkness and confusion the five remaining crewmen and the master had their work cut out trying to keep the *Prymrose* afloat and from being driven on to the treacherous rocky coast of Portland. Pumps were manned frantically but fighting a losing battle as waves smashed over the decks, whilst the gale shrieking through the flapping rigging and broken mast made the long night seem interminable.

Ben lay deeply unconscious in the scuppers, drenched to the skin and totally unaware of the terrible struggle going on around him.

Rallying his depleted crew as best he could, the master kept the ship afloat, and as the long night ended, when the few survivors had almost given up hope, gradually the storm began to abate.

Frozen, soaked and bedraggled, their red-rimmed and salt-encrusted eyes beheld a welcome sight as a watery dawn crept in from the east—a sail appeared out of a final rain squall!

Hopes were raised.

"Courage lads," called the master, "We are saved!" then as the ship grew nearer, blood turned to ice in his veins as he recognized the *Queen of Padstowe* with her murky brown sails, the craft of the infamous pirate, John Piers!

There was nothing the helpless *Prymrose* could do, wallowing in the troughs of waves and making no headway. The few remaining exhausted crew members were unable to prime or aim the cannon and in any case there was no fight left in them. It was just too much. The master's chubby face was drawn as he watched the pirate ship getting nearer and nearer, its intent obvious.

Helplessly they saw the *Queen of Padstowe* come alongside, her yelling crew of cut-throats bloodthirstily brandishing cutlasses.

Flinging grappling irons across to hold the two vessels side by side John Piers and his henchmen clambered aboard. The captain was a cruel and ruthless villain from a wicked family—even his mother was reputed to be a Padstow witch.

"Well, what've we yer?" he cried sliding his sword back into its scabbard when he realised the crew members were unable to put up any resistance, and surveying the damage, "A helpless ship, ready t'be taken?"

"Take the ship . . . but spare my poor men," gasped the anguished master, falling to his knees before the pirate. "They have suffered dearly already! Just take what you will and put us ashore, I BEG you!"

"Aye, I'll spare ye . . . for the fishes!" cried Piers and with a nod of his head instructed two of his men to toss the unfortunate master overboard. They took him, one on either side man-handling him to the rail.

"NOOOO . . ." he yelled, struggling frantically, but weakened as he was from his ordeal he was no match for the pirates as they flung him, kicking, from the ship into the green, foam-topped waves. With a gurgling cry he hit the sea with a huge splash, his face visible, eyes wild with terror then he was swept to his doom.

Piers laughed wickedly, motioning his crew to put the remaining terrified crew members to the sword. Desperately they resisted, struggling and punching their attackers but were easily overcome in their weakened state, and their sorry corpses unceremoniously flung overboard to join that of their master.

Bloodstained decking was littered with pirate spoils. Shouting gleefully to each other at each new find they roistered about the ship, slashing open sacks, plundering goods and carrying off anything they could which was of value and laying waste to everything else.

Piers was having a last look around when he heard a muffled noise coming from a corner of the deck into which a torn fragment of sailcloth had fallen. Shambling over to it he heard a groan.

Kicking the cloth aside with the toe of his boot he uncovered the prone form of Ben, lying on the deck, barely conscious. Blood matted his hair and beard and his clothes were torn, soaking and salt-stained.

"Well, whatever 'ave we found now!" exclaimed Piers, chuckling to himself. A leather wallet was still attached to Ben's belt and the pirate captain bent low, drawing a dagger from his hip and ripping it off. Strolling over to a chest which the men were about to remove he motioned them away and sat on it, his legs in their long seaboots spread out in front of him.

Cocking his head to one side to see better, he examined the contents of the leather embossed wallet which had been given to Ben by Steven's father. In it were some coins which he pocketed and then he found a piece of folded paper.

Opening the soggy document carefully he squinted into the sunlight and laboriously made out the smudged writing. It was the contract the cousins had been given when they signed on for the voyage from Newlyn and proclaimed them to be Cornishmen.

"So ho! Master Benjamin Curnow of Cornwall," he muttered and an impulse prevented him from toppling Ben's semi-conscious body over the side. "No, take him aboard the *Queen*, ye louts!" Whether he spared him because he was a fellow Cornishman or merely on a whim, he didn't bother to ask himself.

So the *Prymrose* was left to her fate on the jagged rocks, wallowing in the foam-topped waves. Yelling to his crew to cast off the *Queen of Padstowe* from the hulk, Piers set his course to the eastwards into the morning sunshine. Screeching gulls circled about her, hoping for fish heads from the cook's refuse pail as he flung the swill over the side.

Below decks Ben stirred painfully. Becoming aware of the salty planks beneath him and that he was on board ship he opened his bloodshot eyes and looked about him. Objects were blurred and out of focus. How he got there he couldn't remember but his head ached abominably. The stale smell of bilgewater surrounded him and he was weak from loss of blood.

Trying to collect his dazed thoughts, to his alarm he found he couldn't even remember his own name! Bewildered, he staggered to his feet and holding on to the side attempted to walk.

One of the pirate crew saw him.

"Your man 'as woken up!" he called to his captain.

"Ah, returned to the land of the living, eh?" chuckled Piers, swaggering over and displaying his blackened teeth in an evil grin.

Ben turned to face him, putting his hand to his throbbing head.

"Sorry, sir," he said gritting his teeth, "I can't remember how I came here, who I am nor what happened!"

Piers threw back his head and roared with laughter. Here is a jest, he thought to himself, I'll play a fine trick on 'ee"

"Why, young Ben, yorr one o' my pirate crew on board the *Queen of Padstowe*" he cried, "You've sailed many a voyage wi' me! You were drunk and fell, 'itting yer 'ead!"

Ben felt sick. "Hell's teeth, a pirate ship—and I'm a member of it's crew! His mind reeled.

Piers clapped him on the shoulder.

"We be returning to Studland now where a welcome

awaits us at the tavern and we'll have another drink or two together—then join the wenches, so you'd best wash that there blood off of yorr face, young 'un!"

He walked away, sniggering to himself at the stricken expression on his victim's face. This could be a sport!

Ben supported himself on the ship's rail, staring unseeingly at the vessel's wake while gulls, echoing his mood cried mournfully.

"Oh God! I just can't remember a THING," he muttered.

Studland was a notorious stronghold of the pirate gangs. They sold their plundered goods at the taverns there and—now that Hawley was taking his percentage—roistered undisturbed by the law.

The strong south-westerly wind carried the *Queen of Padstowe* swiftly along the coast to Studland bay. Once they had rounded Handfast Point with the chalk stacks gleaming in the sunshine, the white-crested waves became calmer in the shelter of the cliffs.

They dropped anchor in the clear waters of the bay in the shadow of the disused blockhouse, sometimes called Studland Castle, and the pirate crews rowed ashore singing lustily, shouting greetings and ribaldry to their comrades on the seaweed fringed shore, taking the confused, injured Ben with them.

CHAPTER 7
Discoveries

The waves could be heard crashing on the rocks from way up the track. Strong winds blew along the channel lashing the dead seed heads of the sea pinks into a frenzied dance.

Coming around the corner to the cliff path, Melchior Strangeways felt the spray blowing off the sea like rain. It was a week since Sarah had been banished from the farm, and he felt both pleasure that his plan for revenge had worked and anger that he could no longer ogle her as she went about her duties.

Making his way carefully over the slippery rocks he salvaged pieces of driftwood from the waters edge.

Something in the trough of a wave caught his eye as he watched the angry sea. He couldn't make out what it was—seaweed or seal? Then unmistakable an arm rolled up out of the water and sank again. A body! There might be pickings! Eagerly he clambered over the rocks. Yes, there were bits of wreckage cast up above the high tide line, recent too by the looks of the new splintered white wood showing on a broken spar.

Looking around he found a length of rope and after several abortive attempts managed to haul the body up on to the rocks, bending down to examine it. The corpse was that of a plump man, he thought, but that might be the result of it being in the sea for a few days, bodies seeming to inflate like pigs bladders after a long submergence.

He searched the body, giving a grunt of disgust as he found nothing of value. The only thing worth salvaging was the leather belt which, although sodden had a rather attractive copper buckle, the like of which he hadn't seen before. Taking it off he looped it over his arm and unconcernedly toppled the body back into the sea to let the waves and the fishes complete their work.

"I'll wear it when it's dry," he said to himself, running the leather between finger and thumb to remove the water.

It was still quite early in the day. His master had dispatched him to the little village of Sandwyche to buy some fish which suited him very well. He intended to combine the trip with a detour over the hill to Studland where his pirate acquaintance, Snivelling Charles awaited him. The man originally came from Lulworth but was now a gunner on *The James*, a Scottish vessel and the two unsavoury characters sometimes drank and wenched together at Munday's tavern.

Returning to the fork in the track where he had tied the pony and the cart Strangeways clambered aboard giving the animal a hard whack, sending it scrambling up the rough path, ears flattened to its head at the stinging blow. The poor animal trotted along the windswept track, head held low and lack-lustre eyes resigned to its weary load.

On past the ancient field strips he went, still defined by their hedges which extended from the highway to the sea, and trundled on through the hamlet of Ulwell over the winding hill-track.

A mile and a half later he arrived at last in Studland.

"Whoa," he bellowed pulling up by Munday's tavern to be greeted by Snivelling Charles, whose name suited him to perfection. He seemed to have a permanent head cold and his clothes were an ill assorted collection, greasy and begrimed which he never bothered to launder, gathered over the years from various prisoners of the pirates.

Melchior still gave the pirates a hand from time to time, absenting himself from the farm for days on end, even sailing with them on occasions, helping them dispose of their goods and taking a percentage of the profits.

* * *

Sitting alone with a flagon of ale at one of the tables, Ben saw the two unsavoury specimens conniving in a corner. Something about the newcomer's belt registered in his mind, had he seen it before somewhere? But it slipped elusively away before he could recapture it.

He still remembered nothing before his arrival at Studland and apart from nursing a splitting headache, was left much to himself with nothing to do, Piers having tired of his sport with the unfortunate young mariner.

Along with the rest of the crew he ate at the tavern, but slept in a rough shed on his own near the shore preferring that to the dubious pleasures of the bawds beds used by his supposed shipmates.

* * *

The body of the *Prymrose*'s master was not the only one to be washed ashore on Purbeck. Fishermen had found other flotsam and corpses, and word was spreading around Poole of the wreck of the once proud ship but news had not yet reached Corfe.

One morning, Steven rode to meet the Ower ferry boat to collect some hangings for the castle hall. Watching the craft draw near to the shore he stood ready to catch the line and noticed the ferryman looking discomfited.

"What's amiss?" he asked, his voice low with concern, tying the boat to a mooring post.

"Bad news I'm afeared, Steven. The *Prymrose* be wrecked and there b'aint no survivors."

He straightened up, feeling the blood drain from his face and aware of a rushing noise in his ears. In his mind's eye he had a sudden vision of Ben as he was on the quay at Poole, saying farewell the night before he sailed for the New Found Land.

"Is there NO hope?" he croaked through lips that didn't want to move, steadying himself. (Oh Ben, young Ben, my cousin and only relative. Are you gone too?)

"Sorry, lad," muttered the ferryman. "Would've 'eard by now if there 'ad bin."

He gathered up the parcel with lifeless hands, putting it across Melody's saddle, slowly leading the mare back along the track and tying her to a tree. He wanted to be alone . . . head in his hands, he sat on a mossy log.

"Why Ben?" he agonized. Life was hard and cruel—the lad was so young, barely nineteen and all his life ahead of him—now this!

Heaving a great sigh he pulled himself to his feet and collected his horse. Life must go on, he realised and with a heavy weight around his heart made his way back to the castle.

* * *

Sarah had been brushing the spiral stairs in the Plukenet Tower. She couldn't explain it, but the place had a peculiar attraction for her, not only for the views that if afforded but for the strange crest she had discovered on its outer wall—a coat of arms of some long-dead knight. There was a normal enough shield with lozenge devices, but on each side were stone gauntleted fingers as though the bearer were still there behind it, petrified in stone, holding the shield aloft for all time.

She glanced out of the window and from the vantage point saw Steven crossing the drawbridge and went running down the stairs to meet him.

"Oh Steven, what is it?" she asked anxiously, gently touching his arm and noticing the lack of spring in his step.

"Ben . . . his ship sank."

"Oh God, no!" she whispered, her face crumpling. She hadn't known his cousin well, but knew how much he meant to Steven. Leading him to a quiet corner of the castle garden she pulled him down to sit beside her on a stone seat, cradling him in her arms like a child, and perhaps it was in that moment that their love was born . . .

They held each other close until he put her from him with a crooked smile.

"You're all I've got now, Sarah."

She suddenly felt that she was the older one, eternal woman, provider and comforter.

"I will always be here, as long as you want me my love," she replied tenderly, stroking his hair and raising the palms of his hard, calloused seaman's hands to her lips, kissed them gently.

* * *

As Steven said, life had to go on. There was much to do at the castle, and in the weeks that followed he worked hard to keep his mind from dwelling on his loss, trying to wear himself out in the daytime to stop the sleepless nights, imagining Ben's restless body in its watery grave.

* * *

One day, he had to ride to Sandwyche for Hawley. There had been a sea fog early in the day but the winter's sun had driven it away. The scent of woodsmoke hung in the air as he strode across the bailey in the direction of the stables to saddle Melody.

"Steven, my love! You walked past me!"

He looked up and she suffered a pang as she saw the dark circles that had appeared under his eyes. Smiling, he came back to her.

"Sorry Sarah, I was miles away."

"Yes, you often are, nowadays," she said ruefully..

"Then I'm a fool!" He straightened his shoulders. "Listen, I'm just off to Sandwyche—is there any chance of getting away and coming with me?"

"I'll ask," she said, beaming at him, "don't go without me!"

She ran back across the bailey and up to the keep where she found Hawley. His face brightened when he saw who it was.

"You're in great haste, my dear. What's the problem?"

"I was wondering . . . Steven has been so depressed lately—since Ben's ship sank, in fact. He's going to Sandwyche for you today and . . . do you think, sir, I could go with him please?"

She looked so pleadingly at him that even his hard heart softened.

"Well, I must admit you have both worked well since you came here, and I believe in just rewards for good service. All right, run along but don't be late back! There is still work to be done, remember."

Her face lit up. "Oh THANKYOU, Master Hawley. I promise we'll be in time!"

He looked after her thoughtfully as she hurried from the room.

"A pretty little piece," he muttered reflectively.

She collected a cloak then ran down the stairs and back across the bailey to where Steven was waiting.

"I can come!" she called.

He grinned at her pleasure, little creases appearing at the corners of his eyes.

"I've spoken to the ostler and he says you may ride one of the horses. 'T'will be more comfortable than both riding Melody—but not as interesting!"

Delighted to see him in such good spirits at last she was determined to help him enjoy the day.

They set out along the valley road riding past the chapel and hamlet of Afflington, through the sunken green lane to Woodyhyde, Downshay and Wilkswood. Flaming trees of the beechwood stood tall as a cathedral and fallen leaves scrunched and rustled beneath their horses hooves, disturbing pheasants that whirred away in alarm.

"Look, Steven," she said, pointing to the yellow leaves in a damp hollow, "they're like gold coins all over the ground. Isn't it wonderful how they come from little buds on seemingly dead trees, open out like hatching butterflies, shelter us from the hot sun then fall and turn back to earth for the tree to grow in again?"

"I didn't know my love was a philosopher," he said, his forehead wrinkled in mock dismay, then becoming serious. "It IS wonderful though. When you see all this around us"—making a wide sweep with his arm—"it makes you realise how insignificant all our little mortal problems are. When we are dead and gone all this'll still be here and other people will ride these tracks, seeing the same hills, valleys and woodland." He sighed. "So we must make the most of the time WE have here."

"Now who is the philosopher?" she smiled.

Chuckling, he spurred his horse. "Come on Sarah, my love, we must call at the windmill with the flour order."

They could hear the grinding of the millstone as they approached Windmill Knap. The sails turned slowly in the gentle breeze and she looked about her while he spoke to the miller. The religious house nearby was now abandoned.

What a waste! she thought, visualising the past splendours, and then he re-appeared.

"That's that done. Are you ready? I've a letter to deliver to Master Henry Wells at Godlingston."

She nodded her assent and they cantered on.

After about another mile they came upon the lovely grey manor house tucked away in its fold in the hills, the Norman tower old even in those days.

"What a lovely house," she said, drawing rein in the gateway, then dropped them on the animal's neck, letting it graze. "I'll wait here while you deliver the letter."

Steven rode up to the entrance, knocked and delivered the message into the hands of a servant.

Sarah sat on horseback watching the clouds float over the hills and thought what a peaceful place it was. Doves murmured from the cote and a cat strolled over to greet her, tail erect like a banner.

Her reveries were interrupted by the return of Steven.

"Nearly done, my love," he said as he rejoined her and they rode off to Sandwyche.

It wasn't far from Godlingston. The small grey fishing village straggled up the hill and huddled around a point in the bay where a little stream flowed into the sea. A group of scavenging dogs ran barking to meet them as they approached then dashed away chasing seagulls.

Presently he halted.

"Hungry?" he asked.

"I'm ALWAYS hungry! Are we going to eat here?"

"There's a tavern that serves fish cooked straight from the sea."

"Mmmm! That sounds delicious—lead me to it!"

They warmed themselves by the fire while the food was being prepared. Steven took the cloak from her shoulders, playing with a lock of her hair and leaving his arm linger around her neck as he unfastened the garment, hanging it over a settle.

Raising her hand to his cheek and stroking his face and beard she said simply. "This is lovely."

"My beard?" he said, deliberately misunderstanding her.

"Well, that too," she countered mischievously. "Oh look

here's the food," and they set to eagerly, silent until they had had their fill.

"What've you got to do in Sandwyche?" she asked, pushing her empty plate away and taking a sip of wine.

"One more letter to deliver—an order for fish for Christmas—and then our time is our own."

"I mustn't be late back, I promised."

"No, of course not. But we will have time for a stroll on the shore if you would like that?"

"You know how I love the sea! Come on, let's go if you're ready then."

Steven paid the landlord, and leaving the horses in the tavern yard they delivered the letter on foot then walked along the sand towards the lofty cliffs of Ballard Down.

A strange whirring yet musical sound came from overhead and looking up they saw five swans banking and coming in to land on the calm bay. Sarah gave a cry of delight and they stood watching the graceful creatures, revelling in their own unaccustomed leisure.

"Do you know," he said turning to face her and taking her hands in his, "this is the first time we've had a chance to talk on our own since you came to Corfe. We've never had the opportunity to really get to know much about each other—I haven't even heard how you came to be with your aunt at Poole!"

"Oh," she said as they moved on, matching his stride then walking backwards, looking at the double line of their footprints following them in the sand. "I was born at Sturminster where my parents farmed. I loved it there, I used to milk the cows, feed the chickens and help mother with the cooking and housework. It was an awful shock when they died. A lot of people in the village died that winter. I was ten years old and the only person who could take me was my aunt, but she didn't really want me. That was when I used to go to the quay and pretend I could sail away on one of the ships. The *Bountifull Gyfte* was my favourite—so you see, there was a purpose behind it all—if none of those awful things had happened I wouldn't have met you!"

He looked at her, his heart wrung. Poor little soul, what

hard times she'd had. He hoped that he could make her future happier and that he was worthy of her love.

She stopped and looked up at him. "And what about you—I know NOTHING of your past except that you are a Cornishman—whatever made you leave?"

He took her hands in his, pulling her down to sit beside him on the soft sand and stared into the distance, lost in memories.

"Whatever made me leave . . .?"

* * *

He and his parents had lived in a stone farmhouse which lay in a fold of the hills above Lamorna Cove. He could see his mother now, a carefree woman, always singing as she worked about the farm, a ready smile for friend and stranger alike. Father, John Curnow, a tall gentle man in the true sense of the word, with grey eyes and a quiet disposition had loved them dearly, never too busy to help him with advice or problems. He had been the youngest son of a well-to-do family, an educated man who had made sure Steven learned to read, and write a fair hand as well.

Pain filled his grey eyes as he recalled the horrific ending to that idyllic time that constantly haunted him . . .

One day he was down at the cove securing his fishing boat against a storm. He had dragged it up the shingle to the high water mark and was sitting, resting on the gunnel when a sudden gust blew over an oil lamp at the farmhouse. The leaping flames could be seen from the cove and he raced frantically back up the steep, winding track but the flames were even quicker.

Mother had been confined to her bed—something he could never remember happening before—a strained back from an awkwardly lifted bucket.

Smoke curled from the roof as he reached the gate when suddenly the dry thatched roof ignited in a ball of flame.

Scorched by the heat he fought his way forwards, calling and shouting like a madman only to be beaten back by the flames.

Snatching a bucket from the wall he doused himself with

water from the stone trough and tried again and again, but the fire had taken hold.

Just before the roof fell in he thought he heard his mother cry "John!" and sobbing, he collapsed on his knees in the farmyard, his hair singed and clothes smouldering.

There was a clatter of hooves in the little lane and a farmer and his son, their nearest neighbours leaped from their cart and began tugging at the blackened timbers. They stopped suddenly, shaken as they came across the two bodies in the ruins of the bedroom. His father had taken his mother in his arms and tried to reach the door. It looked as though they had been overcome by smoke.

There was a shout from the neighbour. Steven lifted his shocked eyes to the place where he stood. A wave of horror engulfed him as he saw a third body. The smell of burnt flesh caught at his throat and he saw a face, blackened and terribly burned. "Oh, GOD!" he gasped recognising the bracelet he had given Becky on their betrothal. They had been childhood sweethearts and were to be wed in two months time in the little village where she had lived alone. She too had known tragedy—her mother died of a broken heart the previous year when her man was lost at sea.

And now there was nothing left! Almost out of his mind with grief, he had left the smoking ruins of the farm and his life and stumbled along the coast to Newlyn. There, he met his young cousin Ben and broke the dreadful news. The two men, anxious to start afresh found the *Bountifull Gyfte* about to sail and in need of hands so had signed on as seamen . . .

* * *

Sarah waited, still holding his hand until he had gathered his thoughts.

Forcing his mind back to the present, his accent more pronounced as it was inclined to be when he was moved, he looked at her.

"I was born in Cornwall, a little place called Lamorna where a pretty little stream runs down a rocky valley to the sea. As a lad I used to pretend I had my own island there—'t'was only a rock, really. I didn't have brothers or sisters either. There was young Ben, 'round at Newlyn though. When I got my fishing boat I'd often see him out in his and we were always good friends. Could say he was the brother I never had, I 'spose . . ."

Making himself continue, his voice husky, "Anyhow, my folks had a farm too. Mother was a happy soul—always singing, I remember. Father taught me to read and write and—well, all about life, really. One good thing, he always had TIME for me, however busy he was . . ."

"Go on," she prompted.

"Three years ago there was a fire," he said bitterly through clenched teeth. "'T'was all burnt, them, the farm—everything. That was when I left Cornwall, met up again with Ben and we signed on with the *Bountifull Gyfte.* We fetched up in Poole—and here I am."

He picked a stone from the beach and threw it into the sea.

"Thank you for telling me," she said in a small voice, frightened by the look on his face.

Deliberately, he changed the subject.

"Do you know, I love that," pointing at the ocean, "The colour of the sea! Look at it, 'tis always different—turquoise over the sand, blue where the sun shines and grey like Cornish slate when 'tis stormy." Picking a spiral shell from the beach he held it out to her. "Put this to your ear and you can hear the sea any time you want." She did, wondering at it, then smiling slipped it into her pocket.

Turning back, he said to her, "And what things give you pleasure?"

She thought for a moment, a little frown creasing her forehead.

"The hills, ships—but not if they take you away—the quiet of the countryside, birds singing, oh FOOD of course, but most of all, being with YOU my love!"

"Oh my little Sarah . . ." his voice husky. "We'd better get back. The sun's sinking low and I don't want you getting into trouble with Hawley."

They made their way hand in hand back along the shore, at peace now, content with just being there, together.

* * *

Not three miles away, Ben went to the shanty by the shore at Studland and laid down to rest. As the moon rose in the lavender October sky the creaking branches of the pine trees made him think of the faint voices of lost children . . .

* * *

CHAPTER 8

Christmas

One morning as the days grew shorter, Francis Hawley sent for Sarah. Combing her hair, she smoothed down her dress and made her way to the chambers that he used as his office.

"Ah, Sarah—come in," he said in response to her knock. He was sitting at a table involved in paperwork which he hated, with untidy piles spread all over the surface. "Now that the preparations for Christmas are almost complete I thought I would have a word with you and see how you are managing. Do you like it here?"

"Yes, sir, I enjoy the work. It is so different from what I've been accustomed to." She looked at him a little apprehensively. Perhaps he would send her away now the work was almost done. Studying his inscrutable face under her eyelashes she could detect nothing so it came as a relief when he rose to his feet and came around to her side of the table.

"Now girl," he said "You can be of assistance. You may have heard of Master Uvedale who lives nearby? His cousin's daughter, Mistress Uvedale is coming to the castle for Christmas and will require a maid servant. Do you think you could cope?"

Her eyes sparkled. "Oh YES sir, I would love to!"

Hell's teeth, she IS a pretty little thing, thought Hawley reflectively, storing the information away for future reference and disregarding her interest in Steven—after all, HE was a far better prospect! Aloud he said, "She arrives tomorrow and will have the chamber on the left at the top of the first floor in the Kings Tower. Make sure it's ready for her. Right—off you go, girl," and he dismissed her with a wave of his hand, getting back to his estate papers. But he watched her covertly as she made her exit . . .

* * *

Christmas was fast approaching and the castle was decorated with greenery—holly, ivy, mistletoe and holm oak. On Christmas Day a fine Yule Log kindled from a piece of wood saved from the previous year's log would be lit, to burn throughout the twelve days in the hearth of the main hall where already the light from the regular fire danced on the wall hangings and tapestries. Hawley's workers had done a first-rate job.

Jane Uvedale came to stay at the castle ahead of the main party. Sarah was rather nervous at the thought of meeting her new mistress in spite of the enthusiasm she had shown to Hawley. Supposing she didn't get on well with her and she was another dragon! However she was pleasantly surprised when she was summoned to her presence.

"Ah, you must be Sarah," said a musical voice as she entered the room, curtsying as she had been instructed. Rising, she saw an auburn haired girl not much older than herself with sparkling eyes and a smile on her lips. Seeing the younger girl's apprehensive expression, she added gently, "Is this the first Christmas you have spent in a castle?"

"Yes, mistress," replied Sarah shyly.

"In that case," looking at the girl's clean but shabby clothes "the first thing we must do is have you dress the part. Here—help me with this chest." She opened the lid, pulling out dresses and flinging them on the tester bed. Holding up two which to Sarah's eyes looked exquisite she said, "Take these. We are about the same height, although I am a little plumper. Are you good with a needle and thread?"

"Oh, mistress!" said Sarah, her voice choked with emotion. She had never before in her life received such gifts!

"Come, if we are to be living in harmony we must be friends. Let us drop the 'mistress' when no-one is around."

She chuckled. "Oh, this is fun—we are going to have such a wonderful Christmas!" Smiling encouragingly she said "Slip the dresses on and I will tell you where they want altering."

Sarah stood in her chemise whilst Jane lifted a woollen dress over her head. It was the exact colour of soft green moss, with embroidery around the neck and cuffs. The sleeves were full, tapering at the wrists, transforming the girl used to poor quality hand-me-downs.

"There, it just wants taking in a little at the waist and it will do nicely. There are needles and threads in that little basket," said Jane indicating where it lay on a shelf. "Why don't you do it now? That will demonstrate two things—firstly what you are like as a needlewoman, and secondly what good taste I have in my companion when you wear it for Sir Christopher's dinner.

"Oh mistress—er, Jane," she corrected at an admonishing look from her new friend. "I couldn't accompany you, I am a SERVANT, not a companion!"

"But Sarah, I have heard Sir Christopher himself say, 'A tradesman can better himself. Men are NOT born equal. If they HAD been, they would have nothing to achieve,' so that goes for a woman too, as far as I am concerned. Come along, let us see to those dresses if we are to have one ready for tonight."

The auburn head and the fair curls bent together over the needlework as the pair worked together, and a bond of friendship was quickly formed. They were both Dorset born and bred. Sarah told of her life on the farm as a child, then with the old woman in Poole and finally how she had spent the last two years in Purbeck on a farm and met Steven again.

"Why, that's fate!" said Jane, then told of her life in her father's manor house in Purbeck and of other Christmases she had spent, very different from those in Sarah's life and the time slid by unnoticed.

Suddenly, bringing them back to the present an excited cry came from the courtyard. The castle with its tall towers on the hilltop commanded a clear view of the surrounding countryside, and Sir Christopher's party had been sighted on the high road between Wareham and Corfe.

Jane hurried eagerly to the window. "Come quickly, we will see them arrive from here," and Sarah pulled a stool close so that could stand on it.

Peering from their vantage point the two young women watched as the party passed the water mill, crossing the stone bridge over the river which acted as a moat and drew rein at the gatehouse just as the sun came out, reflecting on the three rounded domes at the entrance. A rattle of chains announced the lowering of the drawbridge and the group of riders entered.

"There, that is Sir Christopher," cried Jane excitedly, pointing out a well-dressed, tall, graceful man of impressive build with wavy chestnut hair, moustache and pointed beard. Dark eyes flashed from a handsome face. He wore a richly decorated doublet, stiff lace ruff with matching cuffs and a black velvet cap, richly embroidered, sporting a white ostrich feather. A short, full black velvet cloak embroidered to match his hat was flung carelessly about his shoulders.

"The Lord Chancellor of England!" Sarah breathed. She had never seen anyone of such fame and distinction before and gazed entranced. "Who are those people with him?" she asked curiously.

"His page, archer and custrel," said Jane, standing on tiptoe to see better.

"Custrel?"

"Oh—he is a sort of attendant armed with a long sword—see it there? and a demi-lance. The three of them are his bodyguard and always ride with Sir Christopher when he goes anywhere."

Noticing with pride that Steven was holding the head of the Lord Chancellor's white horse, Sarah thought with a warm glow in her heart that he was every bit as handsome as his lord but she was curious to know more about the famous man.

"What sort of person is he?" she asked, gazing from the window. "He must be very grand! I'd never DARE speak to him!" There were ladies and other gentlefolk arriving now.

"Well, he can be really sweet natured at times and as

long as you are not foolish you need have no fear of him. Let me see," she said frowning thoughtfully, "He is pious, a great reliever of the poor, he loves to dance and take part in masques—and he has vowed never to marry because he is devoted to the Queen and she will not have him."

"Goodness!" exclaimed Sarah, her attention drawn from the guests at the thought. "He must admire her very much. I doubt if I could sacrifice my happiness for such a vague hope of love!" As more people arrived she leaned again from the window. "Oh look at the ladies. They must find it very difficult riding in those cumbersome cloaks in the rough countryside!"

Servants arrived to lead the guests to their quarters, their horses taken away and comfortably stabled in the outer bailey. So the castle came to life, torches burning in all of the rooms and courtyards casting dancing shadows on the old walls, while music sounded from the gallery. The Yuletide festivities were about to begin!

* * *

Sarah helped Jane to dress and was amazed at the complexity of the operation: first a chemise smock, then a petticoat of rich material. Next a laced bodice followed by a skirt, French padded around the hips. Then came the kirtle in two parts, bodice and skirt with its long pointed front. Lastly the gown itself which fell from shoulder to heel, open down the front. But she wasn't finished yet, because the high backed ruff and lace cuffs had to be struggled into.

"It's no wonder you started to prepare so early," Sarah said, flushed and laughing from their efforts.

She slipped the green dress over her chemise, saying "I'm glad mine is so simple!" and twirled around making the skirt stand out. Jane smiled at the younger girl's enthusiasm. The old saying was true, there WAS much pleasure in giving!

* * *

The meal was to be served in the spacious and lofty Long Hall on the first floor of the Gloriette Tower. Jane who had visited the castle many times before, led Sarah who had not yet been in this part.

"It will take time for you to find your way around. There are many winding staircases and twisting passages blocked off with closed gates—as means of defence, you see," she explained.

Ascending one such staircase they came through a wide doorway into the Long Hall. Sarah was unable to suppress a gasp at the sight which met her eyes. It was as though a rainbow had filtered into the hall with the bright colours of the fashionably dressed noblemen in their richly decorated doublets, with stiff lace ruffs around their necks and matching cuffs. She had thought Jane's clothes beautiful but they were surpassed by some of the ladies in wide skirted dresses with high ruffs, stomachers and farthingales encrusted with pearls and jewels.

A table stretched the width of the room at the far end with others at right angles forming an 'E' without the middle stroke, and covered with a snowy white damask table cloth set with glittering Venetian glass and silver plates.

The wall hangings were a most impressive sight—green leather, gilded with heraldic devices, stretching some twenty feet to the dim, smoky ceiling. A tapestry adorned another wall depicting forest scenes with wild animals lurking between the trees.

The whole room was decorated with green boughs and lit by oil lamps, giving a soft, warm glow supplemented by the logs burning in the wide fireplace and there was the scent of rosemary and lavender in the air, masking the more unpleasant odours of warm humanity and damp dogs lurking under the tables.

"We all dine here together—Sir Christopher and his guests at the top table, their men and women at the two side tables," explained Jane. The pair took their seats, Jane at the end of the top table and Sarah next to her at the beginning of the side table as the hall filled with revellers.

When they were all seated Sir Christopher hammered

on the table for silence. He was fashionably dressed in a snowy white velvet doublet embroidered in red, with elegant matching breeches and hose and a lacy ruff around his neck, with his beard and moustache pomaded and waxed. When the chatter died down he rose to his feet, his smile encompassing the whole assembly.

"I bid you all heartily welcome to this castle of Corfe and sincerely wish that this Yuletide will be a merry one. We have ordered many and varied entertainments for you which I trust will be to your liking. One thing remains—to announce who will be our 'Lord of Misrule' and will continue in office until Candlemas—and I declare it to be . . ." he paused, "FRANCIS HAWLEY, who has done such a stalwart job in overseeing the alterations to my castle and the preparations for these festivities."

"Francis Hawley!" everyone chorused, raising glasses and tankards in a toast while Hawley smiled with satisfaction at the honour which had been bestowed upon him.

Servants entered carrying a roast boars head with glace cherries for eyes. There were leeks, beet, cabbage, asparagus, parsnips, peas, turnips, beans, onions and spinach with venison and beef followed by marchpane, snap-dragon, mincemeat, cakes and pastries. The best Gascon wine was served and the revellers set to with a will.

* * *

Sarah couldn't see Steven anywhere. She heard someone playing a lute whilst the company was eating, then, hearing 'The Spanish Lady' played in his own individual style, realised it was him. The food was better than she had ever tasted before in all her life but she wished he was sitting next to her, then everything would have been perfect.

At last, when everyone was replete and the meal cleared away the 'Lord of Misrule'—whose word was law while he was in office—summoned Steven to come out in front of the company and sing. Conversations halted as people became aware of his fine voice. Soon Hawley signalled to Sarah to accompany him and gradually the guests joined in with seasonal carols, rounds and ballads.

Pausing for a moment after a particularly jolly sea-shanty whilst the company quietened down, he began the hauntingly beautiful song, 'Greensleeves', looking across at Sarah with a tenderness that left her in no doubt that the ballad was intended for her ears alone.

"Alas, my love, you do me wrong
To cast me off discourteously
For I have lov-ed you so long
Delighting in your company.
Greensleeves is all my joy,
Greensleeves is my delight
Greensleeves is my heart of gold
And who but my Lady Greensleeves . . ."

As she listened, her heart seemed to swell within her. This is one of the good times, she told herself. Hold on to it—life won't always be like this, and unbidden her eyes brimmed with tears.

The last chords faded away then the moment was shattered by the 'Lord of Misrule'.

"Enough of this melancholy, let us tread a measure!" he cried and there was a bustle and chattering from the company as they took the floor and three other musicians came to take Steven's place.

Sarah, at his side now, smiled up at him.

"You sang beautifully, Steven. I was proud of you. But you must be famished?" she added, practical again.

"You sang well yourself—our voices are well matched—like us! And no, I'm not hungry," he murmured, his expressive grey eyes lit by an inner glow.

"If you are sure, may we watch the dancing together? I have never seen anything so grand."

"You are as beautiful as any of them . . ." The young girl from Poole was indeed transformed! "Come, we can watch from over here," and drawing her into a corner he let his hand rest lightly on her shoulder, gently fondling her ear.

They watched the colourful company, tapping their feet to the rhythm as pavane followed galliard.

"Will you do me the honour?" enquired a voice at Sarah's side.

She swung round, seeing the Lord of Misrule smiling down at her.

"Oh no Sir, I cannot!"

"What, after I have given you work and a roof over your head? I must remind you, NO-ONE can refuse the Lord of Misrule!"

She dimpled and shrugged. "But—I have never learned to dance, my lord, so it IS impossible!"

"Then you must LEARN! Our men and women are often called upon to make up sets—is that not true Jane?"

"Oh yes, I will arrange it. Steven, do you dance?"

"I have never had the opportunity."

"Then this is your chance. Tomorrow morning, in my apartments—both of you. Is that clear?"

They smiled at each other.

"It will give us great pleasure," Steven answered for them both, giving Sarah a long, meaningful look.

* * *

The next morning as soon as his tasks were done, Steven presented himself at Jane's chamber. She had arranged for Richard, one of the pages to play the flute for the dance lessons, and so they prepared themselves.

Sarah had risen early and attended to Jane. Then, brushing her hair she put on a loose robe loaned to her by her mistress which allowed freedom of movement and suited her well.

"Well," said Jane, "we'll waste no time. We will begin with a pavane, a slow, stately dance in double time," and explained the steps.

Taking Sarah by the hand Steven bowed to her and lifted her hand to his lips in salutation. They began to dance, with Jane calling out the directions until they had them off by heart.

They moved together with a natural grace, gestures and steps flowing easily. He enjoyed the feel of her lissome body in his arms and she in return the feel of his firm, muscular shoulders beneath her fingers.

She thought she couldn't be happier—she was with the man she loved and he was giving her his full attention. There was a step in the dance where they held hands backwards behind their heads and looked into each other's faces. Smiling up at him with her green cat's eyes she caught him gazing down at her with such longing in his grey ones that she felt her heart fluttering like a caged bird.

"Fine," called Jane, "You are making very good progress so we will now try the corranto. This is a running dance in triple time, if you remember. See how you manage."

Once again they picked it up quickly, having watched the dancers the previous evening and both being blessed with an intuitive sense of rhythm. They found they were really enjoying themselves, Steven letting himself go for the first time since the news about Ben and when the dance ended he swung her round until she collapsed laughing in his arms.

"Oh, I can't ever remember having enjoyed myself as much as this," she said rapturously.

"Well, you've made a good start," said their tutor who was also feeling happy, moved by the pair's obvious enjoyment. "Next time we will do the galliard, which is a gay, zestful five-step and then, if you are still on your feet 'la volta'. All the young people like that one."

"Is that the one where the couples face each other, revolving in circles and the men lift the ladies and swing them off their feet?" asked Steven gleefully, giving Sarah a playful twirl.

"That's the one."

"Until tomorrow then?"

"We can't wait!"

Steven made an exaggerated bow to the two girls and left the chamber. He had business with Sir Christopher, who, exasperated with Hawley's atrocious writing had discovered that Steven wrote a very fair hand and summoned him to transcribe some important documents for him.

* * *

The following day was bright and crisp, so the Lord of Misrule arranged a riding party to exercise the castle falcons. The stables were in the First Ward, just inside the main gates and the party assembled there to select their mounts. Jane rode a quiet grey mare called Dove, and Sarah a bay, Cedric. He was a staid old fellow with a Roman nose, but the girl made him respond having been used to horses since childhood.

Sir Christopher rode out first on his fine chestnut stallion accompanying some of his guests from London. The Lord of Misrule was there of course, cutting a fine figure on his skittish bay whilst his man was mounted on a roan.

Sarah looked hopefully for Steven, but he was still busy with Sir Christopher's affairs and the party moved off without him.

They rode first to the hamlet of Afflington where Hawley had a moiety of the manor, played bowls in the summer, practised archery and where the falcons were housed. Clattering hooves echoed across the stone-flagged courtyard as they collected them from the mews.

Chattering gaily the party rode past the little chapel, turning southwards and taking a boulder strewn track leading to the top of the chalk downs with its breathtaking views. Reaching the top they paused, letting the horses have a short rest then broke into an exhilarating gallop along the ridgeway. Drawing rein to look for prey they scanned the surrounding countryside, the horses' breath steaming in the keen wind.

Taking a falcon on to his wrist Sir Christopher removed its hood, stroking its mobile head. The bird's watchful eyes ranged the hills, absorbing every movement in the undergrowth until the knight released it.

"Go, my beauty!" he called, sending it after a hare that was unwise enough to be out in the open. The hare twisted at the last moment but the hunter anticipated the manoeuvre and the end was quick.

They were having a good afternoon's sport when a lone rider appeared on the hilltop and cantered up to the Lord Chancellor.

Calling, "Excuse me," to his guests he conferred with the

man then rode over to the party and gave his apologies. "I'm sorry, I have to leave you—matters of State to attend to, but I hope you will continue the hunt."

There were cries of disappointment from his guests but he wheeled his horse and doffed his hat in a graceful bow from the waist then cantered away back to the castle with the messenger and bodyguard of page, archer and custrel.

* * *

All the birds of prey were exercised and before long the manservant had hares and rabbits dangling from his saddle. They moved off along the ridge and with the departure of Sir Christopher, Hawley manoeuvred his horse alongside the two young women.

"There," he said, pointing to the north and nudging his horse closer to Sarah until they were riding stirrup to stirrup, "Do you see at the edge of the harbour? The town of Wareham, and further to the east—there, across the other side. That's the port of Poole." He leaned towards her, saying under his breath, "You ride well, girl. I like a lass who can handle a horse—and a man!"

"Now, Francis," called Jane who had overheard him, "You leave Sarah alone. I know what a philanderer you are, but she doesn't." Turning to Sarah she said with a smile, "Beware of him Sarah, he has a beguiling way with him!"

A look of annoyance flashed briefly across Hawley's face but he quickly hid it.

"How you two fair maidens can resist such a handsome fellow as myself I will never understand!" he said lightly, "Come, I will race you to that thorn tree on the next crest," and, his wicked brown eyes a-sparkle he urged his bay into a gallop.

Sarah glanced at him apprehensively but was reassured by Jane's presence and felt that she may have misunderstood him. He couldn't have meant anything—it was too preposterous!

The hunting party rode on until the short winter afternoon was ending and a glorious sunset filled the western sky. Then and then only did they return to the castle, full of high spirits after their ride.

Passing a window Steven heard the clatter of hooves below, looked down and saw the animated group laughing together and was filled with an inexplicable sense of foreboding . . . then his thoughts were interrupted by a servant appearing at his side.

"Steven Curnow?"

He nodded tersely.

"Sir Christopher would like to see you at once."

Damn, he thought. He hadn't seen Sarah since morning but hurried to Sir Christopher's chambers, hoping he would not be detained for long.

"Ah, Steven. I must go to London on the Queen's business and would like you to accompany me. It's a nuisance in the middle of the festivities but it can't be helped. We leave in the morning at first light. There will be much to do this evening–I have more papers I must make ready and then there are my clothes and horses to organise for the journey. It could take us three days to reach London but I hope we can do it in two, it depends on the state of the roads and the weather, so will you make the necessary preparations please?"

"Of course, Sire." He felt honoured at being asked to do such a service after only a short acquaintance-ship and hastened to make the arrangements.

The evening sped past. He didn't have time for dinner so snatched a scratch meal as he worked. His one concern was leaving Sarah, and when it became evident that he was not going to have time to see her he borrowed pen and paper and wrote her a note.

"My love, I write this in great haste to let you know that I leave at dawn with Sir Christopher for London. I have tried to see you this evening to tell you myself, but there has been much to do to plan for the journey and I fear that there will not be time. I will think of you whilst I am away and ask you to pray for our safe return.

S.

Giving the note to Richard the page with strict instructions to take it to Sarah at once, he settled down to the rest of his tasks with a clearer conscience.

The lad sped off, running down the twisting stairs and across the garden. It was frosty on the hill with its weird night noises—the hoarse coughing cry of a stag echoing from the forest—the eerie yapping of a fox carrying across the vale, its bark sounding from a long distance in the cold night air. Shivering, the page hurried to get away from the unknown and into the warmth of the castle when his feet suddenly shot from under him on a patch of ice and he went down. As he hit the ground he put out his hand to save himself, feeling a sharp, sickening pain in his shoulder as his collar bone snapped. He lay there, dazed and whimpering, holding the elbow of his injured arm to support it and to relieve the pain.

Un-noticed, a folded piece of paper fluttered away down the hillside in the darkness . . .

* * *

Sarah and Jane had prepared themselves for dinner with great care and excited laughter.

"Wear the mulberry velvet tonight, there will probably be dancing after we have eaten and you may join in those that you have learned. Sir Christopher loves it. Do you know what was said at Court? 'That it took him twenty years to dance himself into the Queen's favour.' It is quite untrue of course—but nevertheless, Her Majesty IS very fond of dancing!"

The pair hurried to dinner, but to everyone's dismay the Lord Chancellor had sent his apologies to his guests, saying he was busy with matters of State and that the assembled company must start without him.

Sarah repeatedly glanced at the door, waiting for Steven to appear but he didn't come.

The meal over, three musicians played a few tunes, but without the host the evening fell flat and people started drifting away to their beds.

"Never mind," Jane said consolingly, "There is always tomorrow."

Sarah was numb with disappointment. Surely he would have sent her a message if he couldn't come himself? Had she mistaken his feelings for her after all—wasn't she good enough for him now? She lay in her bed looking at the dim ceiling in the moonlight, unable to sleep.

The long night wore on. Oh Steven, Steven, she thought, tossing and turning, I'm so afraid of losing you! Taking the shell he had given her on the seashore she held it to her ear, and drawing comfort from it, listened to the echo of the unceasing swish of the waves . . .

* * *

The following day, Jane sent Sarah to look for Richard to see if he could play for them again. Hurrying to his quarters she was met in the corridor by Hawley.

"You will be having no music from that lad for a while," he said grimly. "The fellow was running around outside last night and fell, breaking his collar bone."

"Oh, poor boy! Is he all right?"

"A trifle feverish and in some pain, but he is young and young bones mend quickly."

"I must tell Steven we won't be having our dancing lessons today then."

"Did he not tell you?" he said, his eyes narrowing. "He left for London at dawn with Sir Christopher."

She felt she had been drenched in ice-cold water. How could he go away like that without even a word to her? She turned from Hawley so he wouldn't see the tears filling her eyes and stumbled along the passageway. A doorway opened out on to a parapet and she went outside, letting the cool breeze soothe her, breathing deeply and trying to compose herself.

Hearing a step behind her she hurriedly brushed away her tears with the back of her hand.

"Now what is this my girl—tears?" said Hawley's voice consolingly. "He is not worth crying for. Anyone who leaves such a pretty partner does not deserve to dance. Come, I have a spare couple of hours and my word is still law. I will partner you! There are plenty more pages we can commandeer, I will see to it."

Jane was not very happy at the solution.

"I'm surprised Steven didn't leave you word of his departure," she said a frown creasing her forehead. But seeing the look of pain that crossed the younger girl's face went on hastily, "He must have been very busy on his first journey with Sir Christopher though and he wouldn't want to overlook anything. I am sure he would have seen you if there had been time. Well, we will see how Francis manages as a tutor."

At that moment there was a knock at the door and Hawley entered accompanied by a dark haired gentleman who Jane had seen at table the previous night. A page followed carrying a lute.

"Ah, Jane. I have brought Sir Hugh with me. I thought together we could dance a set." And also pair him off with you, leaving Sarah for me, he told her silently.

Hugh made a low bow to Jane, sweeping his hat from his head and across his body in one flowing movement.

"It is an honour to be asked to assist two such beautiful ladies!" he said, his brown eyes melting. The room was filled with his vibrant, flamboyant personality. He was so sure of himself, but in such a boyish, charming way that it was impossible to resist him. "I am Hugh de Coursey from Brendon Hall, Somerset at your service."

Jane's eyes sparkled with fun at his mock-solemn, confident approach.

"I suppose we might as well continue, then. We were to do the galliard today and perhaps 'La Volta' if things went well."

"Ideal, My Lady," said Hawley wickedly.

"Come, let us drop this formality. Call me Jane—and you too Hugh."

"'You too Hugh'", echoed Hugh, imitating her. "Ah, Jane, you sound like a wise young owl!" and, the ice broken they laughed together as the page began to play.

* * *

Sir Christopher's party had left early for London. Dawn was breaking and frosted grass rustled beneath the horses hooves like dead leaves.

As the journey was to be made as quickly as possible they rode their own horses hard until they reached Wimborne where they took a brief rest and changed to fresh mounts. In good weather and given a fair road a fit horse could achieve five miles in an hour. Sir Christopher had his own post stations every ten to twenty miles and London was a hundred and twenty miles from Corfe.

They were fortunate in one respect as the frost held all day. Although this made it uncomfortable for themselves it meant the roads remained firm and not the quagmires they could sometimes become. They had spent the first night at an inn on the outskirts of Salisbury and set out again early, stiff at first from the previous long day in the saddle.

"We will try to reach the inn at Basing tonight," Sir Christopher announced when they were changing horses again. "We have made excellent time so far. It's a place I often use—the beds are clean and comfortable and the food is good."

Steven to his surprise found the Lord Chancellor a likeable person. He had imagined someone in that station to be unapproachable but this was by no means the case, the man had gone out of his way to put him at his ease, and apologised for spoiling his Christmas.

"Not at all, Sir. Please God there will be other Christmases but I may never get such an opportunity as THIS again."

They rode into the yard of the inn, weary and travel-stained from a full day in the saddle. A groom came out to take their horses and Steven removed their personal saddle-bags, slinging them over his arm whilst the page carried Sir Christopher's luggage from his pack horse.

Water and basins were brought to their rooms and they gratefully cleansed the worst of the journey from their persons before sitting down to a welcome meal of savory stew.

The young page who had been sneezing on the journey looked exhausted and, excusing him Sir Christopher sent him early to bed, saying Steven could attend on him that evening.

Meanwhile the custrel and archer were catching up with the news, chatting to the landlord who they had met many times before on the way to London.

Sir Christopher and Steven luxuriated in front of a roaring fire, legs stretched out in front, thawing. A bottle of Gascon wine was uncorked between them and the talk ranged from the affairs of the capital to more personal matters.

"You came to Corfe with the young girl who sang with you a couple of nights ago, I believe? A lovely young woman with a good voice," he mused. "May I ask where you met her?"

Steven chuckled, grey eyes merry.

"I've known her since she was a child, some three years ago. She used to haunt the ships at Poole, searching for adventure—wanted t'be a lad and sail off across the seas!"

"That would have been an awful loss to womankind! But still," he said growing serious, "there are fewer barriers for women nowadays—one only has to look to our Sovereign Lady Elizabeth to see what can be achieved by a woman." His dark eyes grew sad and Steven looked at him searchingly. Was it true that he longed to wed the Queen but she wouldn't have him?

Sir Christopher sighed deeply, changing the subject.

"Do you enjoy visiting the playhouse? I'm very fond of the theatre myself." He refilled their glasses and leaned forward, staring into the fire. "Life sometimes seems like a play. Some of us have larger parts to play than others, whilst we slip in and out of life like actors on a stage. We none of us know how long our allotted span will be so it is to our advantage—and indeed our duty—to live each day to the full. There is so much that I would wish to achieve but life is so short, so fleeting that at times it makes me weep."

Steven was moved to see the other, human side of this great man.

"I think it could be said that you have achieved much already."

"But not the one thing I desire above all others—the hand of one who will not have me."

So it WAS true, thought Steven with a pang of sorrow for his master.

Sir Christopher called for another bottle.

"This will take the stiffness from our bones and make us sleep, it's a pleasant beverage," and he waved to Steven to pour another couple of glasses.

"Will you see the Queen tomorrow?" he asked, his mind hazy with tiredness and the wine, then realised he had spoken his thoughts aloud, but Sir Christopher was unperturbed.

"Please God, yes. I should be with her all evening, so you will have time to sample the delights of London on your own. But watch to your wallet, Master Curnow, there are pick-pockets about even at this festive season."

"I'll be careful, Sir."

"Now, I think we had better retire. We've still a long ride ahead of us in the morning." He picked up the half-empty bottle and got to his feet. "Come Steven, give me a hand on these stairs—I swear they get steeper every time I visit this establishment!"

He paused on the landing.

"Have you heard that Elizabeth has nick-names for all her courtiers?" His voice was a little slurred. "You know what she calls me? Her "Mutton"—a play on "Hatton"—God what a woman! And dance—she makes thistledown look heavy!"

Steven smiled to himself. His master should sleep well tonight!

But he was wrong . . .

* * *

Sir Christopher paced the floor of his room, up and down, up and down. No, he couldn't sleep in spite of the wine and his fatigue. Pausing in his pacing he gazed from the window into the moonlight. Mist rose from the fields, and an owl like a white ghost swooped silently from a tree at a small victim, while an errant breeze whispered in the branches outside his window.

Why is it that I'm not content? Why must I always be

seeking for something I cannot have? he pondered. How had this dissatisfaction begun? Searching his mind he thought back to his childhood. His father had been an unimportant Northampton squire. No, he'd been happy enough then. Smiling ruefully to himself he recalled his education at St. Mary's Hall, Oxford and then the Inner Temple.

He nodded dreamily, Yes, that was when it had begun. He remembered one Christmas there. He was twenty-one and had been elected Master of the Games. In this capacity as Student Official he had been responsible for presenting a court masque, 'Gorboduc' before the Queen, and in the performance made up of plays and dances the audience mingled with the cast.

He loved to dance, and was a skilled performer and musician. Elizabeth had admired the handsome young man and they had danced together. She too was a brilliant dancer and their steps flowed with the music.

Yes, he mused, it was the galliard. He had lifted her by her tiny waist, looked into the face of the Queen of England and lost his heart—never to own it again.

He sighed—Well, my beloved Queen, tomorrow we meet and you will break my heart yet again.

CHAPTER 9

Studland

A chill wind blew off the sea that afternoon but as the day wore on it died. Icicles hung from the caves at the edge of the red cliff and the tough grass was stiff with frost.

Studland village resounded to a cacophony of noise from drum, fife, sackbut, cornet and trumpet—Munday's tavern was celebrating Yuletide!

"What's keeping you, boy—more wine!" called Piers and the pot-boy hurried to bring another bottle.

Maria was sporting a bright yellow and green brocade dress. She had been a pretty country girl from Somerset until she took up with the pirates and came swaggering up behind Piers, pushing his hat over his nose.

"Come on Johnnie, let's have a game, 'tis Christmas! What about 'Hoodmans Blind'?"

"Hah—foolishness!"

"If you catch me, you get to—well, kiss me to start with! Don't that tempt 'ee Master Johnnie?" and she ran her finger down his spine, blowing in his ear and making him shiver.

He staggered to his feet, grinning. "Come on, ye scurvy knaves, we be 'aving a game. EVERYONE to join in or they feel the flat o' me sword!"

Pushing stools and tables to one side, ale was slopped from tankards as men none too steady on their feet joined him, ready to take part in the game.

"Who has a kerchief?" called Maria.

Piers pulled one from his neck and threw it across to her.

"Paugh—it's filthy!" she said, screwing up her nose, then saw Ben sitting on his own in a corner by the fire, flames casting shadows on his hollow cheeks. She crossed over to him and stood hands on hips saying saucily, "What about you, Master Benjamin No-Name. Do you have a kerchief?"

Taking one from his pocket he held it out to her without speaking.

"Oh no, sir. You must tie it on me," she flirted, pulling her long black hair to one side provocatively and leaning over him, her low bodice level with his eyes.

"Now spin me round," and laughing tipsily she went off in search of her prey, arms outstretched before her.

* * *

"Someone coming," called the lookout. "'Tis Master Hawley after his cut again and he's got a woman with him."

I've had enough of this, thought Ben. I just don't know what's the matter with me, and slipped out through the side door. He felt sick deep down inside and very lost. Wondering how, where and with whom he had spent other Christmases he made his way to the shanty that he slept in by the seashore. Better company from the sound of the sea than these drunken oafs, he thought.

Through the main door, Hawley entered leading Sarah by the hand, saying, "There you are my girl, you wanted adventure–well, this is the pirates' lair."

Looking about her with some apprehension she saw the tavern women in their spotted finery eyeing her up and down and drew back as one approached her.

"How'd yer like yer fortune told, me lady? Cross me palm with silver?"

"If anyone tells her fortune t'will be me," said a voice from the shadows and a tall, dark woman came forward. "I'm a REAL gypsy, not like these tavern wenches," she said proudly and there was an arrogance about her bearing as the evening sunlight caught the golden hooped rings in her ears.

"How do you do," Sarah replied politely. "I have never had my fortune told–and–yes, I would love to."

The woman gave her a dark, penetrating look.

"Come with me then. We can't do it here with all this noise."

Sarah looked around for Francis Hawley but he was deep

in negotiations with the captains and had forgotten about her for the moment.

Leading her out under the trees away from the raucous tavern, the gypsy woman crossed the lane to a glade in the trees where a spiral of woodsmoke rose lazily into the still air. There, hidden in the trees they came to a gypsy encampment. 'Benders'—tent-like homes made of canvas covered bent poles—surrounded the fire on which something aromatic was cooking in a black pot, and carts stood amongst the trees. Gaily dressed gypsy women watched her under their long lashes as she passed and barefoot children played in the dust with a lurcher pup.

Out of earshot the fortune teller stopped under an old oak and produced a crystal ball from beneath her multi-coloured embroidered shawl, setting it carefully on a log and covering it with her hands. The woman breathed deeply for a few long moments then gazed into it intently taking Sarah's hands in hers. The crystal seemed to smoke and swirl . . .

"You will have an eventful life," she intoned, "Happiness and grief are intermingled . . . I see ships with wide white sails, a far off city and sad partings . . . There is money—and sadness . . ."

"Will I never find true love?"

"Never is a long time and life is short . . . Seek happiness and it could be yours—it is up to you." She studied the crystal ball deeply. "There IS a man . . . I see grey eyes . . . He is looking for something, someone . . . ah! The crystal is clouding. It shows me no more."

Sarah sighed deeply then took a silver coin from her pocket. "Thank you, gypsy. May I ask, what is your name?"

"Golden Hope, my lady."

"Thank you, Mistress Hope. I will remember what you have told me."

She was making her way back to the tavern, fascinated by the dark-eyed gypsy children when suddenly the door crashed open and Hawley lurched out, looking agitated.

"Sarah, have you taken leave of your senses, wandering off like that? This IS a pirates stronghold, remember, ANYTHING could happen to you here!"

"I'm sorry, I was talking to the gypsy, that was all."

"Well, come along, back to the horses. My business is finished for the time being."

He helped her into the saddle, riding his own horse close to hers so his legs brushed against her skirts.

"Have you enjoyed yourself? Are you pleased you came with me? Wasn't I right, you couldn't sit around all Yuletide waiting for Curnow to return. Besides, I am sure he is having fun in London."

"You are probably right," said Sarah with a sigh turning her horse away from his and back towards Corfe.

"Not yet, I must look in at Woodhouse," he called, riding his horse across her path and forcing her to stop.

Somewhat apprehensively she allowed him to lead the way. Woodhouse wasn't far and George Fox would be there, she told herself. She liked him, he was friendly but polite, never offensive.

Hawley turned left off the Corfe road and there in front of them was the house.

"Come, we will go inside, it won't take long," he called holding her horse while somewhat reluctantly she dismounted.

The day was fading but no lights were showing . . . neither was there any sign of his officer.

Opening the door he took her hand, escorting her through with a sweeping bow.

"Welcome to my humble abode," he said bringing her hand to his lips. She caught the smell of spirits on his breath and thought, I shouldn't have come!

Moving into the hall she asked, "Where is the lamp, I'll light it for you."

Suddenly he appeared behind her and she felt his hot breath on her neck. His arms slid around her waist and before she could escape he was fumbling at the fastening of her dress.

"We don't need lights for what I have in mind!" he muttered thickly.

Gasping, she pushed him away, making for the door but he was too quick for her.

"So, you want to play games, my dear! I like a wench with spirit!" he said, his breathing ragged.

Uttering a small cry like a trapped animal she darted back into the room, keeping a table between them.

Stumbling after her, he made another lunge. This time, evading his grasp she almost reached the door but her dress caught on a sharp projection, jolting her to a halt. Tugging frantically she tore free but he was upon her, grasping her wrists in one powerful hand and with the other ripping at her bodice, his mouth crushing her lips, bruising them cruelly.

Frantically she threw him off, desperation lending her strength and picking up a half-filled pewter goblet left on the table, flung it in his face. Rushing to the door she heard him roaring in frustration behind her.

Reaching her horse she leapt into the saddle, kicking him into a gallop, sending the animal scudding up the track towards Corfe.

* * *

It was pitch dark by the time she reached the castle and Jane was amazed to see her coming home alone through the gatehouse, cheeks reddened from the wind.

She ran down to meet her, noticing the torn dress.

"Whatever's happened! Are you all right?"

"It's Hawley," she gasped, getting her breath back, "What a fool I've been!" She had fumed all the hectic ride back from Studland but unwittingly used the anger to cover the deep hurt she felt . . .. Steven was too preoccupied with his new post—he couldn't be bothered to tell her he was going away, and had no time for her. Christmas was ruined and she COULDN'T face Hawley again—what was there to keep her at Corfe? "He attacked me at Woodhouse . . . I'm sorry Jane, it means I shall have to leave here." She flung herself angrily into a chair, elbow on the armrest and chin jutting determinedly. Reaction was setting in now and she felt decidedly shaky.

"On NO . . .! Are you hurt? Did he . . .?

Sarah interrupted. "I was fortunate, I managed to get away . . . he was drunk."

"Oh, thank God for that! But GO? Whatever would you do, where COULD you go?"

"I can go back to Poole. I'm older now, I will find work—cooking, cleaning, sewing. I'll cope!"

"I should never have allowed you to go with Hawley. I WOULDN'T if I'd known, but I was watching the mummers and didn't realise you'd gone until it was too late. Oh, Hawley is a BEAST! He's spoilt everything. I wish Sir Christopher were here!"

"I knew it was too good to last," Sarah said wretchedly, hot tears starting from her eyes. She moved around the room as through sleepwalking, gathering her possessions together.

Jane hugged her. "I'm truly, truly sorry. I HAVE enjoyed your company." Taking a gold piece from her reticule she pressed it into Sarah's hand, saying "You will need money for the journey. Oh, and I must write you a reference . . . Ride Cedric as far as the ferry. I will send a page to collect him—no, a better idea. A page must go with you and bring him back. I'll arrange it first thing in the morning. If you go straight after breakfast you should be away before Hawley gets back. Here, I have a cloak I never wear—take it, it will be cold on the ferry," and pulling a warm woollen cloak from a coffer she hung it around Sarah's shoulders.

Moving towards the door Sarah said dolefully, "Goodbye Jane, you've been very good, a true friend. Thank you for everything. I DO hope we'll meet again."

"Goodbye, Sarah. God be with you!"

They embraced tightly and a muffled sob was torn from Sarah's throat.

Early next morning she collected her horse from the stables and made her way dispiritedly from the castle, feeling more lonely than she had ever done before in all her life.

CHAPTER 10

The Tournament

On Christmas Day, Steven walked alone along London's Strand. Sir Christopher was at Whitehall so he had a few hours to himself, but the city held no pleasures for him. His thoughts were far away in the small village in Dorset, remembering the last time he had seen Sarah, looking lovely in her green dress, reminding himself of holding her in his arms as they danced together in Jane's rooms—the time when they had ridden along the valley to Sandwyche—when suddenly his reverie was interrupted by a cry from above of "Gardy loo!" and a chamber pot was emptied out of the window of an upper storey, rapidly bringing him back to the present. Darting into the road with a muttered oath he was fortunate that the contents missed him, but almost at once it started to rain heavily.

Looking around for shelter, he noticed a tavern on the opposite side of the road and hurried across. It was warm and cheery inside, and calling for a tankard of ale he looked about him.

At a table in a corner a card game was in progress. He wandered over, feeling in need of company on this festive day, noting that the players were made up of three seamen and a nobleman who looked up as he approached. One of the seamen waved at him to take a seat, so drawing up a stool he idly watched as the game progressed, observing that they were gambling, the nobleman obviously losing heavily. One of the mariners winked slyly at Steven then doubled his bid.

"I've no more money on me," said their victim. "Will you take my ring as surety? Just one more chance, my luck is bound to change soon." He was a slim, weakly fellow with small, effeminate hands. Drawing the ring from his finger he laid it on the table. It was gold, set with small but fine emerald.

A gleam came into Steven's eye when he saw it. Immediately he wanted that ring—it was the exact elusive colour of Sarah's eyes and he could just see it on her finger, far more suited than on the hand of this fellow.

"No—us dudn't take jewels. Us only deals in coin, idn't that right, me hearties?"

The nobleman was sweating.

"But my good chaps, you MUST give me another chance to win back that which I have lost," he drawled.

"Can I help?" interjected Steven. "I'll give you a gold piece for that ring."

"It's worth more than that, my good fellow."

"That's all I have, take it or leave it." Steven took a chance on the man's avarice.

"Very well then my good man—you strike a hard bargain."

Steven took the ring and rose to leave, tossing a gold coin on to the table.

"Good luck!" he said, winking back at the seamen, "and a Merry Christmas to you all."

* * *

It was the Tenth Day of Christmas before Sir Christopher Hatton returned to Corfe. Matters of State could take no account of Yuletide and he had important papers to deal with. There had been one glorious evening when he had danced with the Queen but he could no longer make any excuses to stay in the city . . .

* * *

Around the shoulder of the hill on the final bend of the high road from Wareham came a group of riders. The water meadows by the river outside the town were flooded and cobwebs spangled the bushes by the wayside. Riders' cloaks were mud-spattered and horses sweating with the hard ride from their last change over—Sir Christopher, his entourage, and new—albeit temporary—secretary were keen to rejoin the neglected guests.

Steven's grey eyes scanned the castle windows and battlements, his beard and hair damp and curly in the mist, eager for a glimpse of Sarah and to present her with the ring. "For my Lady Greensleeves," he had muttered to himself when parting with the gold coin, visualising her pleasure. It lay now inside his jerkin next to his heart, held by a gold chain that his father had given him which he always wore around his neck.

But there was no welcome at the gatehouse, or in the doorway, or on the stairs to the Kings Tower . . .

Taking them two at a time he raced to the room next to Jane's chamber which had been used by Sarah.

Jane heard the eager steps on the stairs, dreading this moment, and went to the door, pressing her forehead against it and composing herself before lifting the latch, realising she was about to hurt him deeply.

"Steven . . ." she said, haltingly.

"What is it? What's wrong?"

"Sarah has gone back to Poole. Come in and sit down. You must be exhausted after your journey."

"To hell with exhaustion—for God's sake—tell me why . . .?"

Choosing her words carefully she explained what had happened.

Steven's hand flew to his sword.

"By God's beard, I'll kill Hawley," he said darkly, making for the door.

"No you won't Steven," she said, clutching his arm fiercely and restraining him. "You DID neglect to tell her you were going away, you know. How did you expect her to react? She's been dancing with Francis as you weren't there and he may have got the wrong impression. He didn't physically harm her—it was hardly an offence punishable by death!"

"But I wrote her a note! I gave it to Richard—the little wretch, didn't he deliver it?"

"Ah, so that explains why he was running around in the garden the night before you left! He fell and hurt himself but he's on the mend now. The fall must have driven it from his mind."

Steven paced up and down distractedly.

"So she thinks I deserted her . . .! What am I to do, Jane? I can't leave for Poole yet, Sir Christopher has urgent work for me and is to see me within the hour. If anything happens to that girl . . ."

"Don't worry, you will catch up with her again before too long." She smiled tenderly. "You two were meant for each other, you know. Something like this won't keep you apart for ever! Now, SIT DOWN and have some food and drink before you FALL DOWN!"

Wearily he lowered himself on to a coffer which had a soft blanket folded on top, his head in his hands.

"I couldn't live without her now," his voice muffled.

Jane stroked his damp, unruly hair.

"Dear Steven, things will turn out for the best—you'll see. I'm a great believer in fate."

* * *

Next morning, Sir Christopher apologised for his absence and announced that they would resume the festivities with a tournament. The guests were delighted. In spite of Hawley's efforts the party had flagged with the absence of their host—and he was a famous exponent at the Lists.

There were three events: the Tilt, the Tourney and for those who survived unscathed, the Barriers.

The day dawned with a light dusting of frost, changing to a magical golden mist pierced by shafts of sunlight as the sun rose. Word of the forthcoming event had spread around Corfe, and villagers joined the guests, swelling the crowds of spectators and jostling good-humouredly for the best positions. A small grandstand had been erected for the noblemen and women, the ladies sporting 'favours' of their knights.

After the preliminary jousting which opened the gala, amidst rousing cheers Sir Christopher rode into the arena. He was resplendent in his tilting armour, russet with gold bands and lozenge-shaped designs. On his breastplate a figure of Mercury, the winged messenger with two capital 'E's surmounted by a crown, the monograph of the Queen. He was mounted on a black horse with black plumes on its head, and accoutrements to match his armour, the animal dancing on its great hooves, frenzied by the cheers and fanfares.

His challenger was Sir Hugh de Coursey, the flamboyant showman who had been Jane's dancing partner, and he circled his horse in front of the stand, kissing his hand to all the ladies, not content to dedicate himself to one.

The atmosphere was tense with excitement as a herald sounded a fanfare for the competition to begin. Sir Christopher's page slipped the while silk jupon embroidered with the knight's coat of arms over the suit of armour and the contestants took up their positions. The snorting destriers were urged forward into a gallop and with a shock of blunted spears the horsemen met across the 'Tilt'. This was a barrier covered with cloths that ran longways down the centre of the lists to prevent the riders colliding and to keep them in a straight line.

Hawley kept a record of courses run, with marks credited for spears fairly broken or 'attaints' to head or body, and amidst excited cheers from the onlookers Sir Christopher emerged the winner.

Next came the Tourney–this too was fought on horseback with swords clashing instead of spears, whilst in the foot tourney the assailants–local gentry, Haward of Newton, Wells of Godlingston, Clavell of Barnston and Lawrence of Creech–were dismounted and fought alternately with push of pike and stroke of sword across a wooden obstacle.

At last, the main event arrived–the Lists. Excitement and tension ran high as the onlookers waited for the competition to begin. A wind had arisen and its icy blast made the flags and bunting crack and flap, seeking out every nook and cranny of the castle and the spectators stamped their feet and blew on their fingers for warmth.

The Lists were sixty paces in length and forty in width running east to west in the First Ward of the castle and with a 'gate' at each end. The ground sloped somewhat, so the uphill riders had an advantage. The knights and gentlemen taking part were grouped as Challengers and Defendants, whose 'hostages' were placed before the stand, remaining there until redeemed by the valour of their champions.

Sir Hugh, the Challenger arrived at the east gate. Hawley, taking the part of the Constable called out in the tradition of the Lists. "For what cause art though come hither thus armed–and what is thy name?"

In a ringing voice that echoed round the battlements the Challenger replied, "Sir Hugh de Coursey, of Brendon Hall in Somerset. I am hither come, armed and mounted to perform my challenge against Sir Christopher Hatton and acquit my pledges."

Hawley formally identified him in the proper manner by reaching up and opening his visor.

Sir Christopher appeared at the west gate absolutely magnificent in white armour with gilt bands of ornament, between which were strings of roses and knots. This time he was mounted on a white destrier, proudly tossing the matching plumes on its head.

Measuring the combatants lances, the Constable took their oaths for fair combat.

At the sound of a trumpet the knights wheeled their horses, returning to the ends of the Lists, Hugh's horse whinnying with excitement and being answered by Sir Christopher's. Visors were dropped and spurs urged the steeds into full gallop, lances secure in their rests under the right armpit, pointing over the barrier at their opponent's chest.

Sir Christopher's dark eyes glittered through his visor. An expert in this field he noted the angle and position of his adversary's weapon, aiming his own at the vital spot on the shield.

Jane's heart was in her mouth. She was one of Sir Hugh's 'hostages' and uttered a little moan as he was struck fair and square by his opponent's lance, flinging him backwards out of the saddle and on to the ground, the crash of impact sending rooks wheeling from the battlements with harsh cries of alarm. Winded, he lay for an instant, fighting for his breath.

"Do you yield?" The White Knight loomed over him questioningly.

"Nay, Sirrah—I was merely getting used to the ground!" countered Sir Hugh gamely, allowing himself to be attached to a hook and hauled back on to his charger to the cheers of the crowd.

They lined up again for the next round and at the next tilt the challenger managed a glancing blow on the defendant but failed to unhorse him. Then came the final run.

Both knights took their places at opposite, sanded ends of the arena, horses snorting and pawing the ground impatiently. The cheers were tremendous and favours waved by guests and hostages alike.

Trumpets sounded for the last time. Visors were lowered and the crowd became silent—waiting. Horses snorted and blew—then hooves were thundering . . . sending clods of damp earth flying into the air, thundering to the attack and both lances struck simultaneously, Sir Hugh's snapping with a resounding crack, Sir Christopher tumbling the challenger once again from the saddle, where he lay prone on the wet green turf . . .

Cheers grew ragged and then died away as he failed to move. Jane, unable to control herself, broke away from her 'hostage' pen and ran to him, kneeling and cradling his head on her lap, ignoring the saturated grass which was soaking her dress.

Steven arrived at the same time and gently removed Sir Hugh's helmet, as the squire had abandoned his master and run after the loose horse. Brown eyes, dark with pain flickered and opened.

"Oh Hugh, are you hurt?" cried Jane, her face pale.

A brief smile flashed for a moment.

"I wondered how I could win your attention," he joked bravely, then caught his breath and bit his lip as pain surged from his broken ribs. He coughed and blood stained his lips.

"Oh, lie still, you ARE hurt!" she said, her eyes troubled.

Sir Christopher rode over.

"What ails my good Sir Hugh—still testing the ground?"

he cried frivolously. Then, seeing the blood, called urgently for his armourer to gently remove the protective suit and take him to his chamber, concern showing in his face for his friend.

Jane went too, holding his hand anxiously.

"It's painful, but I'll live," he hissed wryly through clenched teeth, "I've done this before, you know!"

"Don't talk. I will nurse you until you are well."

His eyebrows shot up in exaggerated pleasure and he gave her hand an answering squeeze.

"That should be even more interesting than dancing with you!"

"Oh, do be quiet—you will make the pain worse." They had reached his chamber now and the men placed him on his bed. "You must be strapped. Can you sit up?" she asked with concern. A servant brought wide linen bandages and very carefully they eased him into a sitting position and removed his tunic and shirt.

Jane felt the heat rise to her cheeks at the sight of his muscular chest with its fine covering of dark hair. He caught her glance and despite his pain a mischievous grin momentarily flitted across his face. Gritting her teeth Jane inspected his body. Between his fourth and fifth right ribs there was an angry red weal where the lance had struck and she placed a soft cloth on it, supporting his chest tightly with the bandages.

"There now, you must rest," she said ignoring his look and easing him down in the bed. Wiping the blood from his lips she pushed the straight black hair back from his eyes and smoothed his forehead. "I will look in later to see if you need anything."

As she tip-toed from the room she heard a whisper from the bed.

"Jane!"

"Yes, what is it?"

"Thank you!" and her heart lurched as his brown eyes held hers, tenderly, gratefully—lovingly?

CHAPTER 11

Poole

The Ferry steps again—was it only three short years since she had climbed down to the ferry boat, eager to start a new life in Purbeck?

Sarah made her way along the quay, memories tumbling over themselves in profusion. Paradise Cellars, the way to her aunt's old house . . . determinedly she turned her back and took a long, lingering look at the ships. They looked so sad, somehow, tied there when they should be carrying cargoes on the high seas to faraway places . . .

"There I go, day-dreaming again!" she whispered to herself with a smile, picking up her bag and setting off up the High Street, avoiding the mud and rubbish in the road and heading into the town.

She stopped at inns and merchants' houses, asking for employment.

"There's people a-plenty but not enough work to go round," said one inn-keeper. "This stay of shipping will be the death of Poole!"

Night fell, and she still had no-where to sleep until in desperation she asked a kindly widow woman if she would let her share the byre with her house-cow.

The woman agreed and grateful for the night's rest, she woke early and lay in the straw looking up at the dawn creeping through a gap in the roof. Life has gone full circle, she thought, remembering the day she left for Purbeck. What happens next? Watching the sun rise, she contemplated her future but came to a blank then decided to repay the widow woman by feeding and milking the cow. When she had finished, feeling untidy and dirty she fetched a bucket of water from the well and washed herself, picking straw from her hair and clothes, trying to make herself more presentable.

The door opened and in came the widow, carrying a wooden platter with bread and milk for breakfast.

"Did you manage to sleep?" she asked. "I woke in the night and thought of you out here in the cold."

"Oh yes, thank you. The straw was soft and warm and I was very tired—I hadn't much sleep the night before."

"I wish you luck, my girl," said the widow kindly. "I remember your aunt, a hard woman. I wonder how she fared in London?"

"I've never heard a word from her," said Sarah wryly. She thanked her 'Good Samaritan' for her hospitality and feeling refreshed squared her shoulders and set off towards the market. Crowds were beginning to gather and she hadn't gone far when she heard a familiar voice.

"Sarah! Be that really you?"

She turned, looking for the source of the voice then saw the woman pushing her way towards her through the people.

"Joan, oh this is great! I wondered if you were still in Poole and was hoping I'd meet you again. How are you? You are looking well."

"I be grand thanks, girl. I've a place at Master Cloade's still, and 'ee's a very good man. 'Ee don't work me too 'ard and 'ee TRUSTS me, more than that old biddy did!"

They giggled together at shared memories, then Sarah said she was looking for work, and explained how her circumstances had come about.

"Oh, Sarah, you've certainly 'ad your share of the excitement you always wanted. Fancy you dancin' in a castle!" She pondered for a moment. "Still, I might know just the thing for you. Master Meryatt's maid be gettin' wed next week and'll go to live at Wimborne. 'Ee 'asn't settled yet who'll take 'er place. Why don't you go and see 'im?"

"Master WILLIAM Meryatt—of the *Bountifull Gyfte*?

"The very same!"

"Oh, that would be wonderful! He's BOUND to tell of his travels at the meal table—MUCH more interesting than the Bonvilles, where nobody talked at all!" (and a link with Steven, too! she thought cannily).

Joan laughed.

"You an' your adventures! You'll never change, young Sarah. Come, we'll go and see 'im now," and the pair set off along Market Street, past the noisy stalls where bread, fish, butter, cheese, meat and vegetables were sold in glorious, noisy confusion to Master Meryatt's house.

* * *

He remembered Sarah at once.

"You wanted to sail with us, and you liked that grey-eyed Cornishman, Steven Curnow if my memory doesn't play me tricks?"

"That was a long time ago," she answered demurely. "I've got over that now," but she had her fingers crossed behind her back, so it didn't really count as an untruth!

He questioned her about her accomplishments and she showed him her reference from Jane Uvedale.

"Very well lass," he said, having established that she could sew, "I shall be pleased to take you on. My goodwife makes clothes for people. She started when I was away at sea a lot and said it kept her out of mischief. Now folks like her garments so much she still makes them, even though I am here, kicking my heels most of the time. Zounds! but it's frustrating!"

* * *

Sarah was very happy with the family although sometimes, watching the way Walter looked at his wife she would think, it must be wonderful to be cherished like that! The children loved her and would climb on her knee, asking for stories. Willy, the eldest lad, named after William Drake, the first mate on the *Bountifull Gyfte* was never tired of hearing how the English fireboats scattered the Armada.

"I'm going to sea as soon as I'm old enough, and sail with father," he told her proudly, over and over again. One day, when he fell and grazed his hands he told her, "Father says I have the sea in my blood, but it looks red to me, not like sea at all!" and she hugged him to her lovingly, thinking of Steven, if only . . .

The days passed uneventfully. She sometimes saw Joan when she went to the market and asked her the latest news, hoping to hear something of Steven.

"Did you know the Mayor, John Berryman's term of office is soon to come to an end and the new Mayor'll be Master Roger Mawdley? Oh yes, a fair man though but 'ee'll soon 'ave trouble to deal with because I don't suppose old Berryman'll want to get involved."

"What trouble is that?" asked Sarah.

"Well, the gunners of Branksea stopped a poor ole Poole fisherman who'd been trying to take a passenger across from South to North 'Aven. Told 'im 'ee didn't 'ave no right—and 'tis been done ever since folks can remember. Any'ow, one of the gunners 'ad a musket and shot at 'im" The cheek of it! 'Ee missed though and that made 'im so mad 'ee struck the poor man over the 'ead with it! 'Ee came on 'ome and 'is goodwife put 'im to bed but 'ee never recovered and the poor fellow died only yesterday! You might 'ave known 'im, a crabbed liddle man with a grey beard. Always wore a canvas jacket and a woollen cap. No? 'Tis wicked what these yer gunners get up to! Well, I must be off. See you again soon—take care!" and Joan went on her way.

*   *   *

There were times when Sarah longed for the flaming beechwoods of Purbeck where the leaves in autumn lay underfoot like wet gold coins. Late one afternoon she sat on the quay steps looking across the smooth waters of the harbour as it glowed like a pearl with the colours of sunset, thinking of Steven.

Leaning back against the faded lions and griffins she closed her eyes and pictured him as she had last seen him—firm jaw with short, neat beard, his springing brown hair, the little furrow between his eyes when he was concerned about something, his strong arms that held her close to his chest when they rode together to Bonville's on that never-to-be-forgotten day that had changed her life. Then again, only a few weeks ago dancing with him at Christmas and being whirled around in his arms and both laughing together. What was it the gypsy had said—'Happiness and grief intermingled . . . ships with wide white sails . . . a far off city and sad partings'—well, so much had come true. She had also said, 'Money and sadness and a man with grey eyes looking for something, someone.'

How strange life is, she pondered. We have so little control over our destinies. Is it all mapped out for us and we steer our courses like barques, blown by the winds of fate? The sun had gone now and the evening star glowed in the sky. Is that heaven up there, she wondered, or do we make our own heaven or hell here on earth? I wanted adventure when I was younger, but now all I want is to be with Steven, care for him and have his children wherever on this earth he wants to be.

A shout aroused her from her reverie.

"There you are Sarah," called little Willy Meryatt, "I've been looking for you everywhere! It's time to eat and it's fish pie!"

Gathering up her skirts and pulling her shawl around her shoulders she held out her arms to the child.

"I'm sorry Willy, I was day-dreaming again."

"It's almost night, so how can it be a day dream?" he asked, full of questions as usual. "And were you asleep if you were dreaming?" Chattering away, he took her by the hand and they hurried back to the house. Lights shone from the windows and a warm fire blazed in the hearth.

Sarah smiled at Mistress Meryatt, thinking, there is a happy woman. She has her man, her family and her home and is truly content.

Pulling her stool to the table she joined them, eating a slice of fish pie, the warmth of the room after the cold of the outside air making her stifle a yawn.

"You should get to bed early, lass," said Master Meryatt kindly. "You're looking a bit peaky."

"Oh, I've sewing to do yet. I'm fine, really I am."

"You said you'd tell me a story about the stone shield in the wall of the castle and the man turned to stone that was holding it," said Willy.

"What's this?" asked his father curiously.

"Oh, there's a shield on the outer wall of one of the towers. It intrigued me and I made up a story about it."

"Tell! Tell!" cried the boys in unison.

She looked questioningly at their parents.

"All right, when we've cleared away. And you must help, children!"

The table was cleared in record time and they all gathered round the fireplace. Sarah sat on a low stool, knees drawn up to her chin, the children looking at her expectantly.

"One day, many years ago," she began, gazing into the fire, "there was a handsome Prince who lived across the sea. His father the King said it was time for him to go out and see the world, so he went to the harbour to find a ship. He saw one, tall as an oak tree with pure white sails."

"Was it the *Gyfte*? cried the youngest child, jigging up and down with excitement.

"No of course not, silly. It was YEARS ago," put in Willy knowledgeably.

Sarah continued, "The Prince asked the master whither she was bound and he said, 'To the isle of King Arthur.' The Prince went on board and they sailed for a year and a day until they came to some white cliffs. Just around the headland was a beautiful bay—with such clear water he could see the fishes swimming down in its depths—where they dropped anchor. They went ashore in a little boat and the Prince, who was very rich and carried gold coins in his belt, bought a beautiful white horse from a cottager in whose field it was grazing."

The logs settled unnoticed in the hearth as the family sat engrossed in the story, the children's eyes round with wonder, Walter smiling indulgently at his wife over their heads.

"Now the cottager knew this was a magic horse because no-one could ride it, but as soon as it saw the Prince it came and ate an apple from his hand! He had neither saddle nor bridle but mounted it bareback and called to the animal, 'Take me to a castle, I wish to meet a Princess!" The horse galloped so swiftly that its hooves hardly seemed to touch the ground until they came to this beautiful castle on a hill between two other hills. There, in one of the towers was a beautiful Princess with long golden hair, crying "Save me! Save me!" and as the Prince rode into the castle a Black Knight appeared, carrying a black shield emblazoned with five lozenge shapes, one on top of the other.

The Prince drew his sword and they fought all across the bailey, up the tower, through the hall and out on to a tower on the curtain wall. First one seemed to be winning and then the other. Suddenly, the Prince slipped on the mossy steps and the wicked Black Knight dropped his shield, raised his sword above his head with two hands and was about to bring it down on the Prince's head when suddenly the magic horse appeared and he kicked the Black Knight and his shield into the wall where he was turned to stone and he remains to this day, still trying to get out, his hands just visible holding the shield! The Prince ran up the stairs to the Princess who fell into his arms and they were married. The magic horse stayed with them in the castle stables and they all lived happily ever after!"

The small child was sucking his thumb, eyes half closed but Willy was full of the adventure.

"Why was he turned to stone? How could a horse do that? What happened to the ship? Can I go and see the shield one day?"

"You can go off to bed now, young man," said Sarah firmly. "Come along. I'll take you both up and tuck you in."

Walter looked at his wife with a smile.

"She's a rare girl, that Sarah. Full of adventures and stuff. I wonder what it will take to make her grow up?"

"Probably a good man like yourself, my love," said his wife contentedly.

CHAPTER 12

The Salvator

If trade at Poole was quiet, Studland's was the opposite, in fact almost the only English ships to be seen off the coast apart from fishing boats were those of pirates and their suppliers.

Hawley was kept very busy, and his officer George Fox spent much of his time boarding ships in the bay claiming the rights of Queen Elizabeth and Sir Christopher Hatton, although the pirates were getting wise to him. Fearing reprisals, he frequently changed sides, getting more and more involved but managing to profit in the process.

It was becoming a joke in Purbeck and Poole. Folks said you could tell who traded with the pirates, as monkeys and parrots appeared in peoples' houses. Hawley himself had one at Corfe where it swore happily at all and sundry. Branksea Castle had some too, chattering away at the men who fished in the harbour. It was also rumoured Hawley even allowed pirate goods to be stored in the ruined chapel there.

Munday's tavern was thriving. There you could drink, dice and lodge. Thief could cut the throat of thief and no-one would interfere.

* * *

Ben, although he had regained his strength, still suffered from loss of memory. He was pacing the beach, weary of being on shore and contemplating putting to sea with the pirates when a ship rounded Handfast Point, anchoring in the bay. Its eight oared longboat ran ashore, and out stepped the pirate captain Clinton Atkinson. He had spoken to Ben before and the pair had formed a kind of friendship. Clinton, an educated man, was the son of a minister who had fled overseas to escape the catholicism of Queen Mary. He had been a prosperous merchant in London, but tiring of the city, turned pirate for excitement and adventure. Once, when they were sitting together in the tavern he confided to Ben that on his first raid he had actually been commissioned by the King of Portugal, and captured a French ship carrying salt which he had brought into Studland bay. Still a man of fashion, he wore doublets of murrey velvet, lace collars and gilt buttons. Many of the pirates were flamboyant but Clinton Atkinson was known as the leader of fashion amongst the Studland band.

Ben helped him ashore, and he and his men carried the goods up to the high tide mark. There was wine, timber, spices, sugar, rapiers and bibles.

"It was a fine chase!" Clinton told Ben. "We sighted the vessel and pursued her for half a day, catching her at last, cutting across her bows and boarding her."

Ben's appetite was whetted.

"I'm fit again and tired of kicking my heels here on the shore. When you go back to sea, will you take me with you?" blue eyes shining with enthusiasm for the first time since his capture.

Clinton shook his head wryly.

"I would with pleasure but I've business in London with my godfather—did you know he is the Earl of Lincoln?—and I won't be putting to sea for a few weeks."

A voice interrupted, saying "If you're looking for a berth, I'm off at high tide in the morning, I'll take you."

The speaker stood looking at him arms akimbo, picking at his teeth with a splinter of wood. Ben recognised William Vaughan, another pirate captain who had made Studland his base.

Clinton frowned at him warningly but was ignored.

"Aye, I'll sail with you," he answered impetuously, "I've a longing to feel the deck heaving beneath my feet again and taste the salt spray."

"Until morning, then—be ready!" and Vaughan swaggered off, tossing the splinter over his shoulder.

"He's a cruel fellow," Clinton told him. "You'd best wait."

"I can't wait forever. One trip, and see how I fare."
Clinton shook his head ruefully. "You may regret it, lad."

* * *

Morning dawned wet and blustery with a strong breeze blowing along the Channel. With a creak and groan the anchor was raised and Vaughan's ship, the *Mayflowyre* set sail, meeting the waves head-on, bucking and lurching out to sea.

Ben was, literally, in his element, cheeks creased in a happy grin beneath his now shaggy beard, curly hair slicked to his head from the wind-tossed spray. THIS he understood!

Vaughan headed his vessel westwards, past the coast of Purbeck and towards Portland, that great peninsula of stone jutting out into the Channel, a smaller Gibraltar. They beat out to sea, the lookout high in the crow's nest, sweeping the horizon for a sail.

Puzzled, Ben gazed as Portland. Something niggled deep in his subconscious. What was it that had happened here? Had he seen this place before? Fool! he thought, he must have. If he'd sailed with Piers they would often have passed by. The memory eluded him and unable to recall, casting it aside he resumed his mariner's tasks, hauling on the sheets, spilling the slack from the sails.

All day and all night and into the next day they searched for their quarry, zig-zagging across the Channel, when at last about noon there was a sighting.

"Sail-ho!" called the lookout, pointing westward from Portland and Vaughan called to his crew to alter course.

Ben had to admire the man's seamanship. Gradually they overhauled the other vessel until they were within hailing distance.

"What ship are you, and where are you bound?" cried Vaughan.

"The *Salvator of Danzig*, heading for home," came the reply.

"She should be carrying a fair cargo," muttered the pirate captain "although she rides high." Cupping his mouth, he shouted "Heave-to!" to the *Salvator*'s master.

Her master's reply was to hoist more sails, realising he was at the mercy of pirates, but Vaughan foiled him by putting a shot across his bows, calling to his crew to use the grappling irons to stay the vessel.

"I ordered you to HEAVE-TO," he thundered, firing his pistol, hitting the master in the leg.

Giving a cry the man spun to the deck where he lay, writhing in agony. Some crew members panicking, raised their hands in surrender, but four, braver than their comrades drew their swords and made a stand until one by one they too were badly wounded and overpowered.

Swarming all over the vessel the pirates searched her but could find no cargo, only a bag of coins which they took to their captain.

Vaughan counted it out. "Thirty five pounds—is that all! You must have more than this!" he bellowed at the master.

"That is all we carried," he cried gritting his teeth with pain and shaking his head.

"We'll see about that—tie him up!" and three of the pirate crew seized the injured man, spreading his arms and tying him by his wrists to the forecastle. Sweat broke out on his brow as he realised what was about to happen.

Ben bit his lip. This wasn't what he had come to sea for! He moved forward to remonstrate.

"Let 'ee bide, you caint do nothin'!" said one of the crew pulling him back roughly.

Vaughan produced a tightly knotted length of thin rope, tying it loosely around the master's head. The man shut his eyes. Pulling a truncheon from his belt the pirate captain passed it under the rope, twisting it so the knots bit deeply into the man's flesh. His head felt as if it were being cracked like a nutshell.

"There IS no more money," the agonized cry tore from the master, "I swear it!"

Vaughan laughed cruelly, viciously kicking the injured leg, twisting even harder until with a sharp crack the rope broke. The victim's body contorted in a spasm, then mercifully slumped unconscious, his full weight taken by his wrists, blood-streaked face deathly white.

The crew maintained an uncomfortable silence.

"All right then, who wants to be next?" said Vaughan looking around. His attention was caught by the purser. "If ANYONE knows where it is, it should be you!" he bawled, his wicked eyes glittering with vicarious excitement.

He went through the same vicious performance again but the purser, unlike the injured Master was stronger and survived the breaking of two cords before passing out.

Vaughan had a lust upon him now. "Bring me the cook," he shrieked, his voice cracking.

"By God, I've seen enough!" said Ben, his face ashen as he struggled to fight his way through the watching pirates. The same man cautioned him to be quiet, then before Ben could see it coming, swung a quick punch to the point of his jaw felling him like an ox.

"Silly young fool," he said to the surrounding men, "Wants 'is block knocked orf!" The men shifted uncomfortably. They too had seen enough but knew what Vaughan was like when crossed. He, fortunately for Ben was too involved with torturing the *Salvator*'s crew to notice the 'mutiny' amongst his own men.

Spreadeagled on the forecastle, the cook's eyes rolled in terror. Fellow crew members fell to their knees, begging the pirate captain to spare him and to search the ship.

"If you find money, you can hang ME!" cried one man desperately trying to convince him.

"Hah," snorted Vaughan in disgust. "Search the ship again ye dogs, and if anyone finds so much as a halfpenny, make sure he brings it to me!"

They searched. Nothing was found—there WAS nothing.

Vaughan was furious. "Take the master and six of his crew aboard the *Mayflowyre*. Stow them in the hold under hatches, and we'll take our prize back to Studland. There, we'll strip her then I'll hold the ship to ransom! Ha-ha-ha . . .! That'll give 'un something to worry about!"

Ben opened his eyes muzzily, shaking his head to clear it and tenderly feeling his jaw. What in Hades had happened? Looking around at the pirate crew he narrowed his eyes. Why weren't they attacking HIM? Then realisation dawned like a dash of cold water as his memory flooded back. Dazed at the shock of it all, he got to his feet and leaned against the ship's rail, breathing deeply.

"What's wrong, Ben," said the man who hit him, slyly, hoping Ben wouldn't retaliate.

Ben gave him a straight look. "Nothing—thanks!" he said deliberately, realising the man had prevented him from worse treatment. He had the presence of mind to keep his restored memory to himself though, vowing to make his escape at the earliest opportunity.

The *Mayflowyre* sailed back into Studland bay escorting the poor *Salvator*. Ben and the rest of the crew were ordered to strip the sails, munitions and all her furniture and take it ashore. This was a long job, and for eight hard days they toiled morning, noon and night to complete the task with no opportunity for Ben to escape—and for all this time the prisoners were incarcerated in the hold with only a small cask of water and a few crumbs of ship's biscuits between them.

The goods safely stored in the large barn next to the church, Vaughan decided on the next stage and took the longboat out to his ship, ordering the master to be brought on deck.

The poor man was in a sorry state, raw marks from the cord still livid around his forehead and the leg wound bound with bloody rags.

"Now, my good fellow," intoned the pirate captain, strutting back and forth in front of his prisoner, "I am going to grant you mercy!" The man looked at him in disbelief. "You will go to Francis Hawley at Corfe Castle and beg for money to redeem your ship! And if you're not back within twenty four hours with the sum—why, I'll set your ship a'fire!"

The man swallowed, running his tongue over his dry lips.

"How am I to get there?" he croaked, "I can't walk and I don't know the way!"

Ben, listening, saw his chance.

"Perhaps I could help, sir. "I'll borrow a cart from Munday's tavern and I can find my way to Corfe easily enough."

Vaughan looked at him closely. Was the lad to be trusted?

Well, he'd have to bring the luckless fellow back or the man would lose his ship. T'was worth a gamble!

"All right, go about it then," he said.

Two pirates carried the injured man to the longboat and rowed him and his escort ashore. Ben ran to Munday's tavern saying Vaughan was commandeering a cart but it would be back in twenty four hours. Thinking quickly he put straw in the bottom to ease the ride and asked for food for the journey. Maria packed him some slices of pie and a flask of ale, running her fingers through his hair.

"Give us a kiss for that, my lover!" she said invitingly.

"Now now, Maria, I'm in a hurry," and picking up the food hurried outside, hitching the skinny horse to the cart and leading it down to the foreshore where two pirates stood guard over the *Salvator*'s master.

Ben lifted him, making him as comfortable as he could in the farm cart, shook the reins and started off up the track.

"Back in twenty-four hours, mind! or the ship's set a-fire!" called Vaughan, laughing unpleasantly and they jolted off across the hill and up on to the rough downland, every bump of the rutted track bringing pain to the unfortunate master.

As soon as they were out of sight, Ben passed him the food and drink. The man's eyes widened in surprise.

"It's all right, I'm a friend, I want to help you." said Ben.

The master looked at him questioningly. "I don't understand this. How can you be with THEM and be a friend?"

Ben laughed wryly. "It's a VERY long story but in a nutshell, I was captured by John Piers, struck my head and lost my memory. Piers thought it funny to let me think I was one of the crew. I was going to your aid as you were being questioned, when a 'friendly' pirate knocked me out to save me getting the same treatment. The knock on the head restored my senses—so now I'm as keen as you to get away! Now, try to get some rest." He took off his jerkin, pillowing the man's head, who in spite of the jolting fell into an exhausted sleep.

* * *

The cart rumbled on over the downlands and at last Corfe Castle came in sight. Ben pulled the horse to a standstill as they drew up at the gates and climbed stiffly down.

"What's your business?" asked the gatehouse keeper.

"I've an urgent message for Francis Hawley."

"He's away. Won't be back for a week."

"Hell's teeth—we've GOT to see him, it's life or death!"

"Then you'll have to go to Weymouth."

Weymouth!—he estimated it was about twenty-five miles away. Studland was another five back again from here, that would be a fifty-five mile round trip—they'd never make it in the remaining eighteen hours left to them which included the hours of darkness, considering the condition of the master who now had a fever and the state of the tracks. Weather didn't look too good, either. He went back to the cart, his heart heavy.

"Sorry, Hawley is away. I wouldn't put it past Vaughan to have known that and sent us on a fools errand! We'd best spend the night at the inn here in Corfe and go back tomorrow. You're in no state to travel any further and I'll explain to Vaughan what's happened."

The man looked at him in amazement, his face flushed and sweating. "You'd go BACK, after what they did to you?"

"I gave my word. There'll be other chances for me. We must think of your ship and your men."

The master grasped his hand weakly.

"You're a good man, Ben. I hope and pray things work out for you."

Ben smiled, comfortingly.

"Wait there. I'll see if they've a bed at the inn."

CHAPTER 13
Reunions

Steven was sitting across from the doorway, pot of ale in hand, thinking about Sarah and how he could see her again when the door swung open, blowing a cold gust of air into the tavern. Glancing up, he noticed a man had come in. Silhouetted against the daylight there was something familiar about his build. He looked again, then, giving a strangled cry sprang to his feet knocking over a stool, slopping his ale and looking as though he had seen a ghost!

"Ben . . .?" he whispered disbelievingly, "BEN! BEN! by God, it IS you!" and stumbling towards him hugged him tightly, slapping him on the back, over and over again.

"Steven, you old fool! You didn't think you'd got rid of me as easily as that, did you?" said Ben, husky with emotion.

"Wherever have you been all this time? What happened . . .?"

"Later, Steven. I'm not out of the woods yet. Let me get a bed for an injured hostage I have in a cart outside, then I'll explain everything," he said, calling for the landlord then going outside to carry in the master.

Steven followed quickly behind, shaking his head, grey eyes bemused and a broad grin creasing his face.

* * *

Early next morning, the cousins rode back over the downs in the jolting cart with the master who was getting perceptibly weaker, and wincing with pain at every bump. They had cleaned and redressed his leg the night before—he was a brave man but the pain and stress were beginning to tell.

Steven had been adamant. He told Ben he wouldn't let him out of his sight again after his 'resurrection'.

"Let you go back to that den of thieves without me, having had you return from the dead? Oh no, young fellow. They will have me to reckon with this time!"

"But they still think I am a pirate!"

"Well, we will say I am Francis Hawley's representative and have come to explain why you haven't brought the ransom."

"Great idea! That sounds perfectly feasible."

Ben drove the skinny horse along the bumpy track, avoiding the worst places where he could. His cousin eyed him surreptitiously. By God's beard—it was good to have him back! The lad had matured in the couple of months since the pirates attack and he wondered how he had fared. He had only given him a sketchy report the previous evening although they sat up talking into the small hours, once they had put the master to bed.

A groan from the injured man brought him back to the present.

"Not far to go now," he reassured him. "Here, have a drink to fortify yourself," and raising him up he held his head whilst he drank, swallowing painfully.

* * *

The pirates' lookout spotted the cart coming down the hill to Studland and ran through the trees to Munday's tavern.

"He's in sight!" he cried.

Coming to the door, William Vaughan pushed his hat back on his head and stood waiting, legs astride and hand on his cutlass.

"Well," he roared, "Do you have the money?"

Steven jumped down from the cart.

"Allow me to introduce myself," he said, his Cornish burr more pronounced as it was prone to be when he was roused. "I'm Master Hawley's man from Corfe. He's away in Weymouth for seven days so this man," pointing to Ben, wasn't able to meet with him. I've come with him to ask for mercy for this poor seaman. He has no means of paying the ransom and has suffered enough already—through no fault of his own."

"Oh, he has, has he?" glowered Vaughan. "Well he can suffer again! I WILL NOT let his ship sail without payment. Let him try . . .er.. the Mayor of Poole! Off with him!"

"Sir," countered Steven, fighting hard to keep his temper, "his leg is badly injured and your 'questioning' has given him grievous pain. Will you not reconsider—he may not live," he said craftily, "then you will get NO ransom!"

Seeing Vaughan about to explode with anger, Ben interjected "Perhaps if we were to take him by boat the journey would be easier. The jolting of the cart on the rough track didn't help his injuries, sir?"

"Coddling the wretch . . .! Pah, so be it then!"

The master threw Ben a grateful glance.

"How are my men?" he whispered.

"I'll try and find out when I get the fishing boat," he said as he and Steven carried him to the sea shore. Leaving his cousin with the master, Ben noticed the pirate who had punched him, and called him to help drag the boat down the beach into the water. "Are the crew members still in custody?" he asked warily.

"Arr, still in the hold, poor beggars. Ye'd best be quick young 'un. Vaughan's in a narsty mood and could start tormenting them agin!"

"We'll make all speed. Come, Steven. Let's get him aboard."

* * *

The little skiff sailed in through the harbour mouth, past the chattering monkeys and screeching parrots on Branksea, around the Oyster Bank and into Poole. The *Bountifull Gyfte* was moored at the quayside and Steven hailed his old shipmates to lend a hand.

"What's happened to him?" asked Meryatt. Then before Steven could answer cried, "Hell's teeth—it's young Ben! It's good to see you, lad. We'd cast you off as drowned!"

"The Studland pirates have much to answer for," Steven

said harshly. "I'll leave Ben to tell you the whole story. I must find the Mayor," and hurried off to the house near the quay, beating on the door with his fist.

"All right, all right, I'm coming as fast as I can!" John Berryman's old servant woman opened the door. "What's your business young fellow, disturbing decent folks, hammering like that?"

"I've business with the Mayor."

"Well, he's not in!"

"For God's sake, woman—where is he?"

"No need for blasphemy! He's at the Three Mariners of course—Well!" she expostulated as Steven ran off along the street in the direction of the inn. "Young people today have no manners at all!" and shut the door, still muttering to herself.

Flinging open the inn door, he saw John Berryman in his customary settle by the fire.

"Ah, young Steven Curnow! We haven't seen you in here lately. Tell me what've you been doing with yourself?"

Steven held up his hand to stop him. "No time for that now, sir. You are wanted on the *Bountifull Gyfte*."

Dragging the reluctant Mayor away from the fire he held out his cloak, waiting impatiently for the man to move.

"I think I deserve an explanation before I venture into the chill of a January afternoon," said the Mayor. Snowflakes were beginning to fall and a wind was getting up.

"Upon my honour, sir—it is a matter of great urgency or I wouldn't hustle you like this. Please," he said, shaking the cloak, "I will explain as we go."

The two men fought their way along the High Street, eddies of snow gusting into their faces, turning their beards and clothes white before they reached the quay. He finished the story as they arrived at the *Bountifull Gyfte*, where Ben was waiting anxiously.

"I'm sorry," said Berryman, shaking his head. "I'd help if I could, but Poole simply HASN'T GOT the money. Besides, my term of mayoralty is nearly up. How would I account for it . . .? And who is to blame? Why, the pirates of course! They rob our ships, we have losses at sea, loss of goods . . ." and he was off again on his favourite theme.

"We might have known HE wouldn't help," Steven said wearily, leaving him expounding it to Meryatt.

"Then what's to do?"

"We CAN'T take that poor fellow back in this weather . . . Listen, what do you think of this? WE'LL take the boat and say to Vaughan that the master wants his ship back without payment as it has been spoiled and stripped. It just MIGHT work, it's not worth much now as it stands."

"I'm game! said Ben slapping him on the shoulder. "It'll be like old times when we were boys together, out in your old fishing boat in rough weather!"

"Come on then, we've no time to lose," said Steven stifling memories of the welcome with open arms from his anxious parents after such an expedition, "We'll have to run before the north-easterlies."

* * *

But it was an anti-climax when they reached Studland, drenched but exhilarated. Vaughan had heard of a French ship in the channel. Tired of his sport on land, he was keen to get to sea again and agreed without argument to Steven's suggestion. He told the cousins they could sail back to Poole with the *Salvator*'s crew in one of his ships and that he would abandon the worthless vessel at Studland.

* * *

"You don't know who I saw today," said Walter Meryatt, returning home that evening.

Sarah and Mistress Meryatt looked up from their sewing.

"No dear, who was it?" answered his wife.

He twinkled at Sarah.

"Your young Cornishman—with his cousin!"

"WHAT!" she exploded, forgetting she was supposed to have lost interest in him. "Steven—here? And BEN, but . . . but he was lost at sea—are you SURE?"

"Well, the pair of them were on the quay, talking to John Berryman and myself, large as life!"

"Oh, how wonderful . . .! I'm so happy for Steven, they were very close. Are they still here?" she added hopefully, her heart thudding.

"No, gone back to Studland in a small fishing boat in the teeth of a gale—but they'll be all right! Two good seamen, they are."

Disappointed at not seeing them, she covered her confusion by picking up her sewing which had slid unnoticed to the floor. Steven had been here—in Poole and she'd missed him" Still, with Ben alive who knows, he MIGHT come back again, and she continued with her sewing, pricking her thumb, pulses racing and fingers all a-tremble.

* * *

The very next day, a vessel put in to Poole with the *Salvator*'s crew on board. They were cold and hungry but glad to be alive and out of the pirates clutches. Gratefully, the master who had spent the night at a tavern on the quayside thanked Steven and Ben for their help.

"I'd be dead if it hadn't been for you," he said, eyes moist.

"That leg still needs attention," said Steven. "I'm sure Master Meryatt's goodwife would see to it for you, and it's not far to his house."

"You've done enough already," said the master thankfully, but allowed himself to be taken there all the same.

Mistress Meryatt opened the door.

"Oh, you poor man! Master Meryatt told me all about you. Of course you must stay here. Those wicked fellows! Inhuman, that's what they are!"

Sarah, humming to herself was giving the children their bread and milk in the kitchen.

"I like magpies," said little Willy Meryatt, spotting one outside the window and chanting.

"One for sorrow, two for joy
Three for a girl and four for a boy
Five for silver, six for gold
Seven for a secret never to be told . . .
Why does mother call ME a magpie, Sarah?"

"Because you collect things—your bits of stone, shells, feathers, those bits of tarry rope."

"Do magpies collect tarry rope? I like the smell of it. Anyhow, it's not rope. Father calls it caulking. We use it to . . ."

But Sarah was no longer listening. Someone was talking to the Meryatts in the other room—it sounded like . . . could it be . . .?"

The boy prattled on,

"It stops the water soaking through the decks and . . ."

"Shush," she said waving her hand for silence.

Outside, the voice was saying, "If we could leave him here until he can walk again . . ."

Suddenly, a figure hurtled from the back room and threw itself at the owner of the voice, hugging him tightly.

"Oh Steven! Steven—I thought I'd never see you again!"

He clasped her to him, catching Ben's wide grin over her shoulder, one eyebrow raised.

"Sarah—that's no way for a young lady to conduct herself!" said Mistress Meryatt, aghast.

"But we love each other!" she gasped, face aglow with happiness.

"And we intend to become man and wife!" added Steven.

Sarah's green eyes opened wide then she laughed merrily.

"Well, if that was a proposal—I accept . . .! Oh Ben, dear Ben, I haven't said how glad I am to see you!"

"Well, things ARE happening rather quickly . . .! Have you two decided where you are going to live?"

"We haven't had much time to talk about it!" said Sarah sitting down, her legs suddenly feeling weak.

"Come," Meryatt said to the others, "We'll retire to the kitchen and leave these two to make their plans. Ben, will you come through and have something to eat?"

* * *

They stood together before the fire, gazing into each other's eyes. Steven held her hand.

"I'm so sorry my love."

"For what?"

"For going to London and abandoning you like that. You must have thought me an awful swine . . ."

She put her fingers to his lips.

"You couldn't help it, you were so busy. I understand that now."

"I sent you a note, you know—by Richard the page. Jane told me he fell and injured himself on his way to give it to you. He was most apologetic when I questioned him and told me he must have dropped it when he fell."

"My love, how could I ever have doubted you! What a fool I was!"

"Forgiven?" he said looking at her forlornly like a small boy.

"There's nothing to forgive. I'm an idiot!" and kissed him lovingly.

"Now," he said, "I've something to tell you," and he looked at her with eyes full of love, taking her hands in his. "When I was riding around Purbeck for Hawley I saw a little farm near Shipman's Pool. As you know, my parents farmed, and when I was younger I was torn between that and the sea. With the stay of shipping I've been thinking lately, it would be pleasant to settle down in a place like that, the sea not far away. I could still have a fishing boat."

She threw her arms around him.

"Oh Steven, my love! It would be so wonderful to share that with you!" her eyes shining.

Unbuttoning the neck of his jerkin he removed the gold chain from his neck and drew off the emerald ring.

"I purchased this in London—for you, my Lady Greensleeves," and going down on one knee took her hand in his, slipping it on her finger.

She hugged him again, kissing him with all the pent-up love of the past few months.

"There's only one problem," he said into her hair, then held her at arms length. "I don't have enough money for the farm yet. I must find a way of earning it, if you will wait for me?"

"I don't mind WHERE I live, and I would wait for ever, my love! But don't make it that long, will you—please?"

CHAPTER 14

Between Wind and Water

Henry VIII was responsible for commissioning the building of Branksea Castle. More of a blockhouse than the accepted notion it was one of a string of fortifications defending the Dorset coastline. Situated as it was on the island which was only a few hundred yards from the narrow harbour entrance it was in an ideal position to control the movement of shipping—which the resident gunners DID with vigour!

The island itself was of some four hundred and sixty acres, its hills mostly covered in heath, gorse and a few scrubby trees with the castle at the south-easternmost point.

Wal Partridge sauntered out on to the gun platform. It was on the flat roof of the building and from his lookout he had a fine view of the Cales with North and South Haven Points.

Below him in a sheltered spot a monkey chattered, tethered by a light chain around its waist, picking at its fur. On a perch nearby were two brightly coloured parrots, chattering, squawking and scolding. At first sight they looked free to fly away but the pin feathers of their wings had been clipped so there was no fear of them straying.

The gunner scanned the horizon beyond the harbour entrance. No, nothing in sight out there but over the dunes of South Haven he could see the bare masts of pirate craft anchored in Studland bay.

It was for such a ship he was keeping watch although the vessel was now under the ownership of George Fox, Hawley's officer at Woodhouse. Fox had bought her from a pirate captain for forty pounds complete with cargo, asking no questions as to how she had come into his hands and ambitious to make a profit for himself.

Partridge stopped in his tracks. Ah yes, there was a ship, just rounding Handfast Point. He went to the stairs and called down to his brother.

"John, she be in sight. Come you up yer and 'ave a look at 'un. I b'lieve it be 'er."

His brother gave an answering grunt.

"I'll be up in a minnit. Me dinner'll get cold, else."

"Pah," grumbled Gunner Wal, "You be a right ole greedy-guts. You come on up yer when I tells you. I be in charge yer, an' when I sez come, COME dang you!"

John's head appeared.

"I be finished any'ow. No need to get all 'et up!"

Walking to the parapet he leaned on it, screwing up his eyes, squinting at the distant sails.

"Arr, that be she all right. Got a funny ole pig's nose, that ship 'as. I saw 'er at Lulworth afore Fox bought 'un. Be she goin' ter off-load yer then?"

"I TOLD 'ee!" said his brother, exasperated. "Ee's got two cases o' glass fer us an' some other bits an' bobs. Remember, we don't say NOTHIN' to NO-ONE 'bout what 'ee leaves yer. Ee's goin' ter unload the rest of 'is cargo at Goathorn." This was a collection of cottages on the southern edge of the harbour with its own little jetty. "Now you get on down ready for 'er when she comes in. I'll give 'er the signal that it be safe to come a-land."

The small ship with George Fox at the helm came in through the harbour entrance. The tide was flowing fast, carrying her swiftly through the narrow gap.

Fox swung the ship's head into the wind, bringing her smartly alongside Branksea's deep water quay.

"Good day to you, Partridge brothers," he called while Baker, his servant and crewman threw a line ashore to John who hitched it to a bollard.

"Is the Guardian around?" enquired Fox, referring to Chris Anketill under whose jurisdiction Branksea castle came.

"No, 'ee b'aint, neither's 'is deputy Captain Phelips," answered the elder Partridge.

"That's a pity, I've something for him—two stools, a table and a ton of iron!"

"'Ow's 'ee gonna get that over to Almer then?" The Guardian had a house there, not far from Lytchett Minster.

"Do you have a boat going that way? I can't very well deliver it myself!"

"Got one goin' ter Holton, that's not far off—will that do?"

Fox made arrangements for the transfer then looked around, stretching and yawning.

"It's very thirsty work, this ship owning!" he said pointedly.

"Go on, John. What you thinkin' about, not offering the gen'leman a drink! We got a nice drop o' wine yer. Sha'n't say 'ow we come by 'un though!" he added with a wink.

They walked across the barbican over to the castle by way of the drawbridge which hung suspended on chains from two heavy poles, and went inside. There were three rooms on the ground floor, with a chamber over the largest of them which was the hall.

Fox looked around him.

"It's some time since I was here last. I see you've supplemented the ordnance."

"Uh? Whass'at you say?"

"I see you have had more weapons delivered," explained Fox patiently.

There was a huge culverin in the barbican whilst stored in the hall were harquebusses, pikes, bows, arrows, a demi-culverin, a falconet and two sakres.

"Oh ah, an' we got two more sakres up on the gun platform, ready for they Spaniards if they be fool enough to show up again. By God, I 'opes they do—I'd give 'un what for! They people o' Poole don't like it, though. Ever since Sir Christopher 'Atton took over they've bin moanin' an' complainin' 'bout not 'avin control over yer!"

"What's this I hear about you stopping folk crossing the harbour mouth by ferry? People've always done that, ever since time out of mind."

"Can't 'elp that. We be in charge now o' boats goin' in an' out so unless they pays us, it's just too bad, id'nt it? They must take what's comin' to 'un!"

How can you reason with people like that? thought Fox, making a mental note to put Hawley in the picture. These

Partridge brothers were of low intellect and liable to be dangerous. It was worth sacrificing a gift or two to their avaricious natures to keep out of trouble himself. Woe betide anyone who crossed them, though!

"Well, I must get on," he said aloud. "There's a cart meeting the boat at Goathorn and I can smell snow coming—I don't want to get held up."

"What if you be stopped?"

"Stopped—me? Why, I'm Ranger of the Forest," said Fox with a chuckle, "who's to stop ME?"

* * *

The *Salvator*'s master was a bad patient. He needed rest, but whenever he was unsupervised he would be up, trying his leg, worrying about his ship at Studland, thinking of her heeling over to the race of the incoming tide and creaking, cracking and sighing as she sank back into the sand.

Steven promised to see Hawley at Corfe Castle and persuade him to intervene with the pirates, but Poole had been virtually cut off by a heavy blizzard which raged for several days, even the Passage boat failing to sail across to Ower.

As for Sarah, she wasn't too upset by the weather—it meant Steven was confined to Poole and they could spend every available minute together.

The day following the blizzard dawned bright and sunny, transforming all the open spaces to a dazzling white. Mistress Meryatt, a romantic at heart, remembering the time when Walter had been courting her and how difficult it had been to spend time alone together, asked the girl to deliver a cloak to a house at Pitwines. There was no need to hurry, she told her, knowing full well that Steven would accompany her if he had any initiative at all.

He agreed with alacrity and they walked together, listening to the squeaky creak of snow beneath their feet, sniffing the elusive, unmistakable smell of the sea.

"Aah, look at Baiter! The windmill looks as if it's made from sugar," said Sarah, delightedly. Children were having a snowball fight and soon the pair became the target, joining in, laughing, slipping and sliding like children themselves. Stepping in a drift she sank up to her waist and lost her balance rolling over, and Steven flung himself alongside her with a shout, snow dusting his beard and eyebrows. Brushing it off, aglow with happiness she kissed the tip of his nose, and he, laughing held her close to his heart then pulled her to her feet.

"I shall always remember this day!" she said, then a cloud drifted across the sun and Steven shivered. She looked up at him anxiously. "What's the matter my love, are you cold?"

He shook his head.

"Something IS wrong! What is it?" she persisted.

Hesitating, he looked into the distance, murmuring "We're so happy—it almost frightens me, as though we are tempting fate!"

Putting a finger to his lips she whispered, "Don't say any more. We WILL be happy, my love!"

* * *

Walter Meryatt was in the Three Mariners supping his ale and warming his toes by the fire.

"If things don't get back to normal soon I shall have to sell my ship," he said dolefully.

"You'd get nothing for it now, with trade so bad," answered his mate. "Besides, what would you do if you didn't go to sea—and what would I do?"

"William, let's hope nothing comes of it, because I'd never make a landlubber. This sitting around, waiting for things to change'll be the death of me!"

"Could get a smaller ship, I s'pose. I've a copy of Hawley's decree here. Let me see . . ." He fumbled about his person, bringing forth a piece of paper and clearing his throat, began to read:

"'To the harbour and customs officers at Poole,' it says, 'Suffer not any barcke, shippe or vessell whatsoever . . . to passe owt your porte, OTHER THAN IN SMALL VESSELLS from ports to porte onlye within this realm . . .

and if in any casse you shall fynd cawse why, then doo I by vertewe of the aforesaid requyer you to take away the sayllis of all suche shippes . . .'

There you are, a small vessel COULD sail!"

"It's a dashed liberty," said John Berryman. "Branksea always came under the jurisdiction of Poole. Since this Christopher Hatton took over, he thinks he can tell us what to do!"

"How big is a small vessel?" asked Meryatt thoughtfully.

"Well, the *Bountifull Gyfte* isn't THAT big, Besides, the decree doesn't actually give a size or tonnage."

"Who gives permission for SMALL vessels to sail?" the master asked the mayor.

He thought for a moment, scratching his head.

"The Customs Officers, I suppose."

"By God's beard, I've a mind to try it! There's a load of copperas from the Parkstone mines waiting to be transported to London. Fellow by the name of Phillipe Smythe keeps on asking when it will be delivered. Says he'll pay well, too!"

Drake jumped to his feet.

"You mean to sail? Do I get the crew together?"

"Why not!" cried Meryatt, the joy at the thought of action infectious. "I've had enough of sitting here on my backside!"

Berryman laid a cautionary hand on his arm.

"You'd better see if you can get a permit first before you call up your crew."

"No sooner said than done!" exclaimed Meryatt, slapping his thigh. "Are you coming with me, William?"

"I'm with you!" said Drake, grinning, ready for action at last.

"You're no relation to that other fellow called Drake, by any chance?" joked Meryatt. It was a long-running jest between them!

The two men hurried off down the High Street, squelching through the slush thrown up by passing carts and entered the Customs House.

Collector Richard Sidwaye was on duty.

"What can I do for you Master Meryatt?" he said, looking up from writing an entry in his ledger.

"I've a cargo of copperas to ship to London for Master Phillipe Smythe. Will you give me a permit?"

"You intend sailing the *Bountifull Gyfte*?

"I do, sir. I've read Master Hawley's decree—no doubt you have a copy? It says 'small ships may move'. Well, my *'Gyfte* isn't VERY large and the document doesn't stipulate a size. Besides, I won't be leaving English waters."

Sidwaye consulted with his Controller and Searcher. They took their copy of Hawley's decree and went through it line by line, arguing back and forth while Meryatt and Drake paced up and down impatiently, eager to be under way now they had set their minds to it.

"What size is the *Bountifull Gyfte?*" Sidwaye asked.

"Well . . . she's eighty foot long . . ."

The Customs Officers consulted again. Drake nudged Meryatt. Richard Sidwaye was writing on a sheet of paper, and when he had finished, called his colleagues to witness it with their signatures.

Sanding it, he came across the room and handed it to the master.

"Right, here's your permit," he said.

The seamen exchanged triumphant glances. Meryatt thanked him, took the paper and once they were outside, read it aloud to Drake:

"'To the Gooner att the Castle of Branksea—

Thes are to let you to understande that the bearer hereof, Walter Meryatt, master of a barke called the *Bountifull Gyfte* bound for London, laden with copperas for Mr Phillipe Smythe hath entered into bonde here to dischardge ytt at London.

Thes are to praye you to p'mitt here to pass withoute any your lette or molestaciones.

From Poole this XIth of February 1589
Richard Sidwaye Collector
Nicholas Symson Comtroller
Robert Gregorye Searcher'

"We've got it! We can sail! He's dated it for tomorrow!"

"It could be dangerous—you'd better warn the crew before they sign on."

"I'll pay over the odds! Master Smythe said he would pay ME well if I delivered. Damn, it'll be good to be at sea again! Drake, you get the cargo loaded and I'll explain to the crew. Ha! I bet young Steven would sail with us. He needs the extra money if he's to be wed."

Meryatt found his crew in the alehouses and taverns along the quayside. At first Steven hesitated, reluctant to leave Ben as they were trying to get the *Salvator* restored to her master but, thinking of Sarah he agreed to sail. The money would come in useful—and it was months since he had sailed on the *Bountifull Gyfte*.

Breaking the news to Sarah that evening when she had finished work was difficult though . . .

"Will it be safe?" she asked. "I'd rather have you alive and poor than rich and dead!"

"Of course it's safe! Master Meryatt has a permit issued by the Customs Officers," he said, minimising the danger for her sake.

"When do you sail?"

"They are loading the ship today and we leave on the morning tide."

"You WILL take care, won't you? I shall miss you while you are away. How long will it take?"

"A week or ten days, depending on the winds."

They sat silently for a while, then Sarah held both his hands in hers.

"I've been thinking. I've a gown to deliver to Haven House tomorrow. From there I could go on to the Cales at North Haven, but I couldn't stay long because I must look after the children in the afternoon, Mistress Meryatt is going to her sister's at Heckford. If you're not too late, I could watch you pass and wave goodbye."

"I shall look out for you. Come, my love—give me a kiss to speed me on my way . . . what's this, tears?" He took her in his arms and wiped them away tenderly. "It won't be for long, then we'll be together all the time."

"I know you love the sea," she sniffed, "but I'll be glad when you're a farmer!"

He ruffled her hair affectionately, thinking how lucky he was to have such a lovely young woman who cared for him.

"Well, I must be off," he said, bending to kiss her and hugging her tightly. "We have to be aboard early to catch the tide," and reluctantly, apprehensively she let him go.

* * *

The quayside was bustling next morning. A sudden thaw meant the snow had gone, leaving the morning washed clean from the heavy overnight rain. News had spread that the *Bountifull Gyfte* was leaving port and a group of townspeople had come out to watch her as she prepared to sail. There was a light breeze coming off the land and the crew clambered aloft making ready to get under way. Soon the salt wind was whistling through the rigging as they pulled out into the main channel.

It was already getting colder again and Sarah wasn't at the quayside. She didn't want to say her farewells in public but left early to take the gown to Haven House in Luscombe Valley. On the way she paused on the headland and saw the ship leaving the quayside. Hurrying to deliver the gown so she wouldn't have to carry it to the end of the sandbanks, she knocked on the kitchen door which was opened by the maidservant.

"Come in lass, and warm yourself," she said and Sarah looked longingly at the large open fireplace, cheerful and welcoming, with bacon hanging on nails to smoke.

"I won't stop thank you. I have another errand," She MUST see Steven if she possibly could!

The *Bountifull Gyfte* sailed proudly onwards, dropping anchor off the castle of Branksea just short of the savage rip tide at the narrow harbour mouth, her topsail furled and mainsail hanging slack in the light breeze.

Sarah scrambled up the rough track at North Haven Point and stood hands on hips, getting her breath back, looking out across the harbour of Poole. As she watched, three men lowered a boat from the ship and rowed towards the castle.

'They are taking the permit ashore,' she thought. 'A pity, they may be some time,' and turned to walk back to the town, glancing over her shoulder every so often to see if they had returned.

She had not taken many paces when the creak of oars carried across the still harbour, and narrowing her eyes she squinted into the pale sunshine, trying to identify the oarsmen.

The three men reached the ship—it wasn't very far—and climbed back on board, the crew hastily making ready to sail.

Her mind wouldn't accept what happened next—like a small white cloud a puff of smoke issued from the castle, followed by the delayed crack of a sakre shot!

Sarah uttered a wordless cry, standing as though paralysed, hand pressed to her throat. Petrified, she watched as a distant figure on the ship removed his hat, waived it in the air and hailed his company.

"Hoist the main topsail!" He commanded, and the rattle of wooden parrels as they slid up the mast echoed across the water to her straining ears while the crew hurried about their business.

The gunner, seeing his first shot had missed, fired off a second sakre which he levelled between wind and water. The shot fell short, skimming over the sea like a stone and bounced, striking the ship at deck level.

Two men fell mortally wounded, and for a tense moment there was a deathly silence until terrifyingly their agonized cries carried across the water.

She gave an anguished moan—"Oh my Steven—my love, please God NO, not my Steven!"

Slowly, very slowing the ship came about and headed back to port whilst on shore the woman ran towards Poole on leaden feet, her breath coming in painful gasps, tears coursing unheeded down her cheeks . . .

* * *

On Branksea, the Partridge brothers, seeing the *Bountifull Gyfte* getting under way had decided to shoot. John fired the first shot, missing the vessel. Wal, the elder brother fired the second shot, then jumped up on the castle wall.

"I can't see for smoke but I b'lieve I've hit 'un!" he cried.

"Yes, it struck the barque and I think you done some 'arm," called back Peter Peers, another of the garrison.

"Yes, I 'ave!" yelled Wal as the smoke cleared, then said nervously to himself, "I can't 'elp it now." As John came and joined him he added "I'm sorry that any man should be 'urt by me—but 'ee DIDN'T 'ave a warrant from Master 'awley—what else was I to'do?"

"What's to do NOW?" said his brother. "There'll be trouble wi' Poole!"

"I must stay 'ere. I'll row you 'cross to South 'aven point first though and come straight back. You'd best go on to Corfe and tell Master 'awley what's 'appened. There'll be 'ell to pay!"

John Partridge buckled on his sword and dagger, his mind in a whirl. We were in the right, he thought then remembered that the decree had said 'take away the sails,' not kill the mariners! The sea was choppy and neither spoke on the short journey, each busy with his own conscience.

"Come back as soon as 'ee can and let me know what 'ee says," called Wal as John landed.

About half a mile along the heather clad peninsula he met Richard Barbar, a workman going back to Branksea from Sandwyche.

"Hello there Partridge! Goin' ter be a rough evening I reckon. Where're you off to then?"

"Corfe Castle. Y'know Meryatt and Drake of the *Bountifull Gyfte* of Poole? They've bin grievous 'urt by a shot from Branksea Castle!"

"Well I never—that'll be trouble! Who shot 'un then?"

"Can't stop now. I gotta see Master 'awley," and he hurried on his way. It was a long journey, about six miles and an icy sleet fell intermittently, cutting like grape-shot.

The castle gates were barred and he had to knock until someone came to open them.

"Who are ye and what's yer business?" called the gatekeeper.

"John Partridge, gunner from Branksea and I must see Master 'awley right away. Two men bin injured bad!"

"Come on in. Here Richard, take Partridge to Master Hawley's chambers."

The gunner followed the page across the steep outer bailey, over the bridge which had replaced the drawbridge, up the staircase, through the King's Tower and across the courtyard to the Gloriette where Francis Hawley was working.

"Master Partridge, gunner from Branksea to see you, sire."

Francis Hawley was in a foul mood. Word had got around that he was condoning the conduct of the pirates and questions were being asked in high places. Unless he did something about the pirate problem soon there would be trouble. But if he DID, his own income would suffer.

"What is it, Partridge?" he asked testily.

"Master, Walter Meryatt and William Drake made to sail the *Bountifull Gyfte* out of Poole without a permit so we fired on 'un."

"Well?"

"I said we FIRED on 'un, sire."

"I heard you, man! What do you expect me to do about it?"

"Well—they was grievous 'urt, sire" the man said uncomfortably, wringing his hat in his hands.

"Get away with you—I'm busy" grunted Hawley, his mind on other things.

Partridge backed out of the room and was taken to the gates by the page. He didn't know what to think—Francis Hawley was in a strange mood, there were no two ways about it! Better get back to Branksea, he thought, although the afternoon was drawing in and he had a good three hours trudge on a rough track ahead of him.

Setting out at a fast pace he soon overtook surgeon Nycholas Purserye heading in the same direction.

"Ah, John Partridge, my good fellow! Who has been hurt at Branksea? The gatekeeper at Corfe told me someone was injured so I thought I should go there."

"'Tis no use you going on, master. T'was Meryatt and one of 'is men, sore 'urt by a shot from the castle. But they was carried back to Poole on the *Bountifull Gyfte*.

"My word! And you've been telling Master Hawley! What did he say to that?"

"Well, master, he did say little to it—'twas rather strange!"

"I'm wasting my time then if they've gone to Poole. I'll get back to Corfe. Safe journey!" and turning about he headed back to the village, leaving Partridge to travel on, alone with his thoughts along the darkening fringes of the harbour.

* * *

The Bountifull Gyfte arrived back at Poole before Sarah, once-proud sails hanging slack and the mainmast splintered. People stood in groups on the quayside, talking and arguing about what had happened.

"STEVEN!" she called hysterically, "STEVEN, where ARE you!" running frantically from group to group.

A tall figure detached himself from a crowd outside a tavern, his shirt bloodstained and a bloody cloth around his head.

"I'm here, my love—it's all right!"

"Oh, thank God, thank God!" Her heart lurched and she fell into his arms not knowing whether to laugh or cry. Everything was turning black. I WON'T faint, I WON'T! she told herself firmly, exhausted as she was after her hectic race against time, then gradually the darkness faded and she looked up. Oh joy! He was still there, his heart beating next to hers, holding her in his arms and comforting her. Then she saw the blood.

"You're hurt!" she cried, her voice full of concern.

"It's nothing. A flying splinter of wood from the mast cut my forehead. The blood on my shirt . . . isn't mine."

She caught her breath. "Who's . . .?"

"Meryatt and Drake. They were both terribly injured. Drake died on the way back and Meryatt when we brought him ashore."

Her face crumpled. "NO! oh no! This is terrible news, those poor, poor families," she whispered. "I was at North Haven—I saw two men shot . . . oh Steven, I thought one was you!"

There was a tug at her skirt.

"Where's my father? I can't find him—or Uncle Willy. It's father's ship, why isn't he here? Why has the *'Gyfte* come back—and why are you all bloody, Steve?"

Grey eyes met green in consternation. The child didn't know! Mistress Meryatt was visiting her sister—so she probably hadn't been told, either!

"Come here, lad." Steven took the boy by the hand, bent down and sat him on his knee putting his arm around the child's thin shoulders. The boy looked up into his face, trustingly. "There were bad men out there at Branksea Castle . . ."

"Pirates?" interrupted the child.

Steven shook his head sorrowfully. This was the worst thing he had ever had to do in his life.

"No," he went on, grim visaged, "These blackguards are worse than pirates. They fired on the *'Gyfte* . . . Willy—I want you to be very brave . . ." He cleared his throat, husky with emotion. "Two men were killed by the gunners of Branksea today. Uncle Willy . . . and your father."

The boy got to his feet, his face chalky white and stood stock still. Swallowing hard, he tried to control his lower lip which was beginning to quiver.

"I was going to sail with father when I was a bit older—now I never will," he said in a choked little voice.

Sarah gave a cry, falling to her knees beside him and hugging the fatherless child to her heart.

"Will you look after Willy, I must find his mother," muttered Steven.

"Of course I will. She is at Heckford."

Steven got to his feet, swaying as he did so.

"You ARE hurt—let ME go," she beseeched him.

"No, your place is with the child. I'm fine—really. I'll ride there, my horse is in the stable."

* * *

Mistress Meryatt heard the horse's hooves galloping up the road to the cottage and hurried to the door with her sister.

Steven slid to the ground still clad in his bloodstained shirt and breeches in spite of the chill day—his jerkin was covering the dead face of this woman's husband.

He fumbled to find the right words to break the news when, with icy calm she said, "It's Walter, isn't it?" her face ashen.

Steven nodded, his grey eyes dark with pity. "And William Drake, too Mistress. The gunners of Branksea . . . I'm SO sorry! They were both good, honest men . . ."

Her sister put a shawl around the bereaved woman's shoulders. "You will be wanting to go home—I will come with you," she said.

Numbly the widow asked, "What of the children—do they know?"

"Willy does, and Sarah is with them now."

"Yes, but they will need their mother. I must go home. Come, sister—and thank you for coming Steven. It can't have been easy for you."

"Will you both ride on Melody? I can walk."

"We have the mules, thank you Steven, we will go on those," said the sister. "Oh dear, my hands are shaking so!"

"I will ride with you. Let me saddle your animals," he suggested going to the stable at the rear where the mules were dozing comfortably. His head was swimming—he had made light of his injuries to Sarah but he'd lost a lot of blood. Taking a deep breath he led the mules outside and helped the women mount.

CHAPTER 15

Retribution

Steven sat at the table in the Meryatt's kitchen. Upstairs the children were in bed while Mistress Meryatt and her sister were in the solar with Sr Symon Berwyke, Curate of St James's arranging the funeral for the following day.

"Something must be done," said Steven wearily.

"Sit over here by the light and I'll see to it," Sarah replied pouring hot water into a bowl.

"No, I mean about those Partridge brothers." He went on almost as though he were thinking aloud, profoundly affected by the deaths of his shipmates, going over the events again and again in his head. "I rowed ashore with Drake and Meryatt. The gunners read our permit and asked if we had one from Hawley. Meryatt said we hadn't, but as we were a small vessel the one we had should be sufficient."

He paused, forehead wrinkled, remembering. "Partridge said, 'Don't you know the last time I let you past, Hawley was angry with me?' but still we rowed back to the *Bountifull Gyfte* and made ready to sail," wincing as Sarah removed the bandage from his head.

"I'll bathe it with salt and water–if salt keeps food good all winter it must have healing powers," she said practically.

Steven muttered to himself, reliving the tragedy, "We left Wal Partridge on the top of the castle. I think that was where the first shot came from and that one missed us. Gunner John was in the lower round..." His face flushed with sudden anger, and hitting the table with his fist he cried, "I don't know who fired the second shot but by God, they are BOTH guilty of murder as I see it!"

Sarah finished rebandaging the nasty cut on his

forehead. She was shocked to see white bone showing through the blood when she bathed it but the edges of the wound didn't seem inflamed, so she fervently hoped there was no infection.

Pushing himself to his feet, restlessly he began pacing the room.

"It was horrific. Meryatt had a huge wound on his right thigh. The bone was shattered. Drake had a belly wound. There was blood everywhere. His voice broke. "We couldn't STOP it!" Glancing down, he saw Sarah's white face and was full of remorse, tenderly taking her in his arms.

"What a brute I am, telling you all this! I'm sorry my love. I can't seem to get it out of my mind—I keep seeing it happen, over and over as though it were a nightmare . . . would that it were!"

* * *

When John Partridge left the castle of Corfe, Hawley felt one of his headaches coming on. What was it that fellow was on about? he asked himself belatedly, Meryatt and Drake—both popular figures in Poole, as if he didn't have enough trouble with the town already. Hell's teeth, 'grievous hurt' the fellow had said! He hoped it wasn't as bad as that! These fellows always exaggerated! Still, better follow it up in the morning or there'd be more trouble. Good job Sir Christopher was away at his estate in Northampton!

There was a knock on the door and the page announced, "Master Nicholas Currey, come for a permit, sire."

"Ah, Currey. A pass for your ship, you say? A pity MERYATT didn't come to me for one. Yes, I'll admit I'm sorry he and Drake were involved but it's too late now."

"'Too late,' the saddest words in the English language. Aye, 'tis a pity, Master. Good men, both of them but I'd have thought the pass they had from the Customs Officers of Poole would have been sufficient for the gunners?"

"No," said Hawley, "If my signature's not on the pass, those gunners, why—they'll tear your ships to pieces! Well, here's YOUR pass. That will get you through all right."

Master Currey squinted at it, thinking, If they can read your writing, that is! and bowing, left the chamber.

Hawley decided he'd better set the wheels in motion, realising that once Sir Christopher in his role of Lord Chancellor was aware of the incident he would convene an Admiralty Court to try the brothers.

Summoning two of his men, Captain Stephens and Henrye Brown to go to Branksea the following day, he instructed them to investigate the affair.

"Find out exactly what happened and bring those Partridge brothers back here for trial," he commanded.

They set off early in the morning, leaving their horses at the stables at South Haven and were rowed across to the castle.

By then news of the deaths had spread and Captain Stephens was perhaps the wrong man to be in charge of the investigations. He had known Walter Meryatt well, often drinking with him at the Three Mariners.

Wal Partridge caught the line from the boat, holding it steady while the two men stepped ashore in stony silence. They walked to the blockhouse still without speaking.

"Nice day," said Partridge nervously.

Captain Stephens turned on him, face blazing with anger. "Whore's son murderer! Have you killed honest mariners?"

The man trembled.

"Aye—'twas a mishap, I'm sorry Captain!"

"SORRY!" thundered the Captain. "Mistress Meryatt and her childer are SORRY, so are Mistress Drake and her babes!" You and your brother are to accompany me to Corfe where you will stand trial!"

* * *

The Coroners Inquest was held next morning, and the Poole court brought in a verdict of wilful murder against Wal Partridge. There was no love lost between Poole and Branksea. The two victims had been popular in the town, and rubbish and filth was aimed at the prisoners as they passed.

That afternoon, the funerals were held at St James's parish church. A great crowd turned out to say their farewells to two of Poole's sons and to mourn with their families.

The youngest child had been kept at home with Mistress Meryatt's sister but little Willy Meryatt stood straight beside his mother as the coffins were carried into the church by Steven—his head still bandaged—Ben and others from the crew of the *Bountifull Gyfte.*

Sarah stood with Mistress Meryatt who was as pale as death, staring straight ahead at her husband's coffin.

The curate, Sr Symon Berwyke conducted the service, calling down the wrath of God on those who molested honest seamen going about their business. He prayed for the souls of the departed and their bereaved relatives then turned to face the congregation.

"I was talking to the Customs Officer Richard Gregory the other day. We were checking through some of his records when I came across the following lines which someone had written, and I pray they may comfort those left behind," and he quoted them in his deep, sonorous voice to the silent congregation;

"'Looke where the tree doth fall. Lo, there it lies
O happie fall, that to the Lord doth rise.'

And the tears which so far had been contained, welled up in Mistress Meryatt's eyes until they flowed faster and faster, her shoulders shaking with grief, recalling the happy times at home, their visit as a family to Woodberry Hill, and the strong arms of her man, never to hold her again.

Sarah put her hand on her shoulder comfortingly, then a little voice spoke through his own tears at her side.

"Father was brave mother, and we ought to be brave too—he would want us to—but I DO miss him!"

"Of course he would, my sweeting," said his mother, taking a deep shuddering breath, trying to bring herself under control. "We WILL be brave," and held the hand of her son tightly whilst the cortege filed out of the church to the burial ground.

* * *

Sir Christopher was at his chambers at Hatton Garden in London when he was told of the killings.

"Those fools have overstepped their mark this time," he thundered, his face grim. "Hell's teeth—it's SPAIN that is the enemy—not our own mariners! Was anyone else hurt?"

"One other, a mariner named Curnow, Sire."

"Not STEVEN Curnow?" rasped Sir Christopher, his eyes narrowing, remembering vividly the dedication and honesty of his temporary secretary.

"I believe so, Sire."

"Well man, what were his injuries . . . were they serious?"

"A head wound Sire, but he soon recovered."

"Thanks be to God!" muttered Sir Christopher. "Has Hawley arranged an Admiralty Court?"

"He has it in hand Sire, and has requested me to carry your commission back to Dorset."

The Vice Chancellor took pen and paper and wrote out the commission. Sir George Trenchard was to preside and the trial was ordered to take place as soon as possible.

* * *

The morning dawned raw and foggy. The towers of the castle of Corfe were lost in the swirling dampness and the grasses of bailey and keep were stiff with frost. The Court was to be held in the Long Hall as a number of people had travelled from Poole to see justice done.

The company assembled and rose to their feet before the Commissioners as they solemnly took their seats. There was Sir George Trenchard of Wolfeton the Deputy Lieutenant of Dorset, John Williams of Tyneham, Edward Lawrence of Creech, Robert Napper of Dorchester, John Browne sheriff and Francis Hawley.

A whispering and jostling spread through the spectators as the prisoners were brought in and stood in the dock.

"MURDERERS!" shouted a Poole voice and was taken up by others while there were more mutterings and threats from other friends of the victims.

Sir George hammered on the table for silence.

"The Admiralty Court of Purbeck has been convened in

this the thirty-fifth year of the reign of Our Sovereign Lady Queen Elizabeth, upon the deaths of Walter Meryatt and William Drake, master and mate of the *Bountifull Gyfte* of Poole on the 11th of February 1589. Accused of their murders are Wal and John Partridge, gunners of Branksea." He turned to the dock. "Wal Partridge, are you and your brother John Partridge gunners and keepers of the castle of Branksea?"

"We are, Sir."

"You are charged with the murders of Walter Meryatt and William Drake by unlawfully discharging a sakre from the castle of Branksea on 11th February this year. How do you plead—guilty or not guilty?"

"Guilty, sir."

"John Partridge, how do you plead?"

"Not guilty, sir."

"Call the first witness."

"Call Steven Curnow."

Steven took the stand, tall and pale, recounting the horror of that fatal day.

"Master Meryatt fetched a permit from the Customs Officers of Poole the day before, the Tuesday. We sailed the *Bountifull Gyfte* to Branksea roads and anchored there while I rowed Meryatt and Drake ashore to deliver the warrant into the hands of Wal Partridge. He read it and asked if we had one from Master Hawley. Master Meryatt said we hadn't and the gunner said he couldn't accept it, so he replied, 'I pray you good Wal Partridge, let me pass and the warrant shall be sufficient for you.' He again said it wouldn't do." Steven paused and visibly controlled himself before continuing. "Master Meryatt said, 'Come on lads, we've given him a permit. Poole Customs are behind us, we can come to no harm.' We rowed back to the *Bountifull Gyfte* and were making ready to sail when a shot was fired from the castle. We were hoisting the main topsail when a second shot was fired striking our ship between wind and water." His voice dropped.

"Master Meryatt and William Drake were struck and mortally wounded. Willy Drake died almost at once and Master Meryatt when we got back to Poole . . ." His tone grew bitter. "T'will be many years before this is forgotten. They were both innocent men, merely trying to earn a living—there was no call to KILL them!"

The court room had been hushed throughout his delivery, experiencing through Steven those terrible moments. But with his final words, as he returned to his seat a clamour of protest broke out and Sir George had to call for silence.

Christopher Jolliffe, another crewman from the *Bountifull Gyfte* was called and though not as articulate, confirmed Steven's statement.

"Call Hewe Graye."

The mariner took the stand, twisting his hat in his hands.

"Hewe Graye, were you on the Lytle John of Poole, anchored at Branksea at the time of the shooting?"

He cleared his throat noisily before answering, "I were, sire."

"Tell the court in your own words what you saw."

The man fidgeted, running his finger round the collar of his shirt, unused to speaking before so many people.

"Well, sire, I did see them fellows from the *Bountifull Gyfte* row ashore to Branksea, but what they did there I can't say, not bein' there myself, like. But after a bit they comes back, rowin' out to the *Bountifull Gyfte* and do make sail. They be under sail when a shot comes out 'a the castle and overshoots 'un. Then I do see the master put off his 'at and shout to 'is company to 'oist the main tops'l and then they gunners shoots another piece of ordnance out'a the castle and that do graze the water and go smash into the barque at deck level, 'ittin' the two men."

There were mutterings from the body of the court and someone shouted "Disgraceful!" but Graye wasn't finished yet.

"Ar'ter a bit, one of they Partridge brothers, dunno which, brings a passenger aboard the Lytle John. I ses to'ee, "Do 'ee know you'm killed two men in the other barque of Poole?" and 'ee do say, "T'was their own follies," then 'ee goes back to Branksea and takes 'is brother over to South 'Aven point and sets 'ee a-land there, but whither 'ee went after that, I dunno."

All those present knew the area and could visualise the

scene. Some shook their heads sadly at the thought of their friends' untimely deaths.

"Thank you, Graye. You may stand down . . . Call Nicholas Currey."

Currey came forward and took the stand.

"Are you Nicholas Currey, master of the *Bonaventure*?"

"Yes sire."

"Were you at Branksea Castle on 11th February 1589?"

"I was, sire."

"Tell me in your own words what you saw."

"Well sire, I was at the castle, Branksea castle that is, after the shots were fired and I was talking to Wal Partridge. He said he was sorry Meryatt and Drake were killed but that he was the man that did it. Then later on I was at the other castle, Corfe, to get a pass for my Barque from Master Hawley. He told me HE was sorry too that the men were killed and I told him I thought their pass from Poole would have been good enough, but he said t'wasn't . . ."

"Is that all, Currey?"

"Aye, sire."

Richard Barbar was called next and took the stand.

"T'was a Wednesday, as I remember it," he said, screwing up his face thoughtfully. "I was comin' 'ome from Sandwyche where I'd bin at work and as I was comin' 'long South 'Aven t'wards Poole 'bout 'alf a mile from the point I met John Partridge. 'Urryin' along, 'ee was with 'is sword and dagger in 'is belt, like. I ses to 'im, "Where you goin' then?" and 'ee ses, "Corfe Castle", then ses 'ow two fellers off the *Bountifull Gyfte* 'as bin shot. So I ses, "'Oo shot un then?" but 'ee didn't say, just 'urried on, like, so I comes on 'ome then."

Several more witnesses were called and all repeated the same story.

A sensation was caused when the defence asked if Wal Partridge who had admitted firing the fatal shot could have 'Benefit of his Book,' a centuries old custom to exercise leniency by admitting the criminal to 'Benefit of Clergy'. It applied to people of 'education' being exempted from the penalty of death if they could prove they could read.

Sir George called again for silence. When the court had quietened down he explained that the felony had been committed on the high seas, so 'Benefit of his Book' did not apply.

The crowd breathed an audible sigh of relief and the jury retired to consider their verdict. The crowd was in no doubt —the Partridge brothers were guilty and must hang!

The atmosphere was tense as, their verdict considered, the jury filed back into the court room and took their seats.

"How do you find the prisoners, guilty or not guilty?" asked Sir George.

The foreman stood up.

"We find John Partridge not guilty and Wal Partridge guilty of manslaughter."

"Wal Partridge," said the Deputy Lieutenant solemnly, "You will be taken to Dorchester prison and there you will remain until it is decided whether you be hanged or pardoned."

CHAPTER 16

The Farm

Steven burst into the house like a tornado. It was April and a sudden heavy shower of hailstones lashed against the windows, matching his mood.

Sarah was at the table with Widow Meryatt, working on a gown for the mayor's wife. The dressmaking had been a godsend, keeping the widow's mind occupied and from dwelling on her grief.

Startled, they looked up.

"What's the matter?" asked Sarah anxiously.

"It's Hawley. I can't get any sense out of the man!"

"What's he done now?"

"It's what he HASN'T done! I've asked him over and over again about the tenancy of the farm but he'll never give a straight answer. I've just seen him on the quay but he boarded the Ower ferry with the excuse that he was in a hurry and couldn't discuss it." He paced up and down, his face flushed.

"Calm down, my love. He won't be hurried." She stood up and poured him a drink.

"I must ride to Corfe and corner him there. If he doesn't want us to have the tenancy why doesn't he say so and get it over with?"

"Because it's not his way to give a straight answer." She thought for a moment, frowning. "He could be doing it to be awkward, paying me back for thwarting him, I suppose—should I go with you, do you think? Perhaps I could persuade him?"

He shook his head.

"No, love. That would only make him worse. Anyhow, it's more likely to be some scheme he's hatched up with a crony of his, I fear."

Widow Meryatt looked up from her sewing. She had aged ten years in the last two months.

"You are both welcome to stay here as long as you like, you know that."

The young people glanced at each other. Steven came around the table and sat beside her, resting his hand on her shoulder.

"You have been wonderful through all this dreadful business and we thank you for your offer. But we would dearly like to start afresh on a farm we could work to our own satisfaction, and we intend to get it." He stood, having reached a decision. "I'll ride to Corfe tomorrow."

* * *

Hawley wasn't at all pleased to see him.

"I told you I would LET you KNOW!" he shouted. "I've more important things to think about than your little tenancies!"

"But it won't take more than five minutes of your time. I've written a rough agreement to save you the trouble. I've done them before for Sir Christopher. If you want to alter anything I will see to it and have a fair copy made. What more can I say?"

Hawley sprang to his feet, knocking against the table and spilling the ink.

"By God's beard, Curnow, you overstep your mark. I've had enough of you. I'll do things when I say so and in my own fashion. Go on, clear out and let me get on with my work."

The door opened.

"What in Heaven's name is going on here?"

Hawley stared in dismay. There stood Sir Christopher, arriving unannounced.

"Sus-sus-Sir!" he stammered, I wasn't expecting you!"

"Clearly!" he answered stonily. "What is the problem?"

"Er . . . nothing I can't deal with, Sir," and he shrank from Hatton's withering glare.

Ignoring him for the moment the Lord Chancellor crossed to Steven, meeting him for the first time since the tragedy, raising his hands to his shoulders and holding him at arm's length for inspection.

"Well, my boy . . . what can I say? I feel responsible for the deaths of those two good men and for your misfortunes, due to the incompetence of my officers," glaring at Hawley. "There are widows and children too, I hear . . . How are they coping?"

"They have houses in Poole, Sir, and the townspeople are doing what they can."

"I believe you have helped as well."

"The men were my friends and colleagues," he said simply. "They would have done the same for me."

"I know it is no substitute for their tragic losses, but I will ensure that the families never go hungry. It is the least I can do . . . and what of you, Steven. What will you do now? There will always be a position for you in my household if you so wish, either here or at Holdenby."

"That is very generous of you, Sir." Then, seizing the chance to press home his advantage he went on, "But what I really want is a tenancy of a farm here in Purbeck for Sarah and myself."

"Sarah—the pretty young lass who sang here at Yuletide?"

"The same, Sir."

"You have excellent taste!" he said with a benevolent smile, brushing a speck of fluff from his immaculate sleeve before asking, "This farm—have you a particular one in mind?"

"Yes, Sir. It overlooks Shipman's Poole and is farmed by an old widower who wants to leave."

Hawley's look could have killed! He had promised the tenancy to a friend of his and would have had his pocket lined nicely for his trouble.

"And is it one of which I am landlord?" enquired Hatton.

"It is, Sir."

"Then it is yours! Hawley, arrange for the lease to be transferred to Curnow's name immediately!"

"Sir, I thank you kindly—but I would rather agree the rent before I sign my name," Steven interjected.

"I should have remembered you are a sound businessman!" said Sir Christopher wryly. "Well, as a gesture of compensation for your injuries . . . will you agree to having it rent free for the first ten years then a peppercorn rent after that?"

Hawley's face was a picture! A nice little income had just been snatched from under his wily nose!

Steven on the other hand was overjoyed.

"Sir, this means everything to us," he said, his eyes aglow. "Now nothing stands in the way of our marriage!"

"Then allow me to be the first to congratulate you!" He took a purse from his belt, removing a handful of gold coins. "Let this be my wedding present. I'm sure there will be things to buy!"

"You are too generous Sir Christopher . . .! Would it be presumptuous of me to invite you to our wedding, if you are in these parts?"

"I should be delighted! Let us hope the affairs of state are kind and do not keep me away. Notify me as soon as you have arranged the date." He turned to Hawley, saying darkly, "When the tenancy agreements are drawn up I will sign them myself. That way there can be no problems."

Hawley scowled behind his back then called for a servant to mop up the ink.

Bowing his thanks, Steven left the room grinning to himself. All the obstacles had now been removed—he must ride back to Poole immediately and tell Sarah!

Yes, God does move in mysterious ways, he thought as he mounted his faithful Melody and swung away from the castle gates. If poor Walter and William hadn't been killed this wouldn't be happening, and he was saddened that his pleasure should be bought at the expense of others. So it was in a more sober mood that he rode through the forest towards the town of Poole.

* * *

A few days later they were walking on the quay, looking at the ships and making plans.

"I still think June would be best. I have to make my gown and bed linen. There is much to be done."

Steven smiled indulgently.

"Well, as long as it's EARLY June. That would be about six weeks. Is that long enough for you?"

She looked up at him questioningly.

"Am I being TOO unreasonable?"

He gave her waist a squeeze.

"You haven't even seen the farm yet. Shall we ride over tomorrow and see what needs to be done? There are no animals on the land, the old man didn't restock after the winter, so we will have to buy our own beasts in due course."

"Go and see it tomorrow? That would be wonderful, my love." They paused in their walk, arriving at a sad sight—the *Bountifull Gyfte* tied up by the quay, her mast still splintered and decks deserted. "Poor *'Gyfte*—she was so beautiful. I wonder what will happen to her?"

"Widow Meryatt is putting her on the market, I believe William Greene and Nycholas Currey are interested. A shame, but it's doing her no good rotting here." He sighed, grey eyes troubled. "Young Willy was so full of sailing on her with his father."

"Come, my love. It's no good dwelling on the past. What's done is done, and we must look to the future."

He straightened his shoulders.

"Dear Sarah, you're so good for me! Well, tomorrow Purbeck, then?"

She smiled into his eyes.

"And our new home! Yes please, Steven!"

* * *

They rode out on a bright April morning to the liquid song of a blackbird, the wayside path dotted with primroses and celandine, and the woods carpeted with a haze of bluebells. The sheltered spots concealed drifts of violets, only revealed by their sweet fragrance. Emerging from the trees they saw the conical hill of Creech looming from the forest where a delicate tracery of silver birches displayed uncurling green leaves, until they came at last to the Corfe road.

"I remember the first time I saw the castle from the carriers cart," she said pensively. "Little did I know what part it would play in my life!"

They made their way to Afflington, then up the track and over the crest to Hill Bottom, pausing to water the horses at the stream, then, leaving the hamlet behind rode around the bend to Shipman's Pool.

Steven drew rein, pointing across the valley.

"There," he said proudly, "our new home."

The farm house and buildings were on a small plateau a third of the way down the hill. The clear stream flowed along the valley bottom, spanned by an old stone bridge, and a thrush poured out its heart in song from one of the apple trees. On the western side were the fields, enfolded in the arms of the hills. It was sheltered from all except the gentle southerly winds, and to the north-east the hills stood one behind the other, concealing the track to Renscombe.

Away in the woods a yaffingale called . . .

* * *

The old yeoman had gone to live with his sister so the house was empty when they arrived. Built of Purbeck stone it appeared to lean in to the hill on which it stood.

Sarah put her head on one side.

"The roof's crooked," she said with a chuckle, "and the doorway isn't quite straight—but see how the doorstep is worn from all the comings and goings it has seen! Oh, Steven—it's LOVELY! We're going to be happy here, I KNOW it!"

They went in. The house was one whole room wide—the kitchen, with a narrow pantry running along its length. Through the kitchen was the heart of the house—the dining room and living room combined. There was a fireplace almost the length of the wall with a little bread oven built into an alcove. All the ground floor was of stone flags and Sarah was already picturing it with rag rugs by the fireside.

She flitted from room to room like a butterfly.

"How many bedrooms are there?"

"Do you know, I never thought to ask. I haven't been upstairs. Still, if there aren't enough for you I can always build on," he said with a twinkle in his eye.

Catching his hand, she led him up the stairs. There were two bedrooms, the larger looking out over the sea.

"This is heavenly! I can just imagine us in our advancing years, sitting here watching the sea, the children coming home from their voyages and telling us where they have been—oh my love, I can't wait!"

The twinkle became a gleam.

"You can't . . .?"

She blushed.

"We'd better go downstairs—you're beginning to look wicked! It won't be long now until we're wed—oh, it IS difficult!"

He opened his arms and she ran into them, melting against the length of his muscular body.

"Come now lass," he said gruffly. "I don't have a will of iron! I know you believe I won't take advantage of you, but holding you like this—I find it very difficult."

"My love, I'm so sorry!" she said, dimpling. "Come—let's look at the farm buildings. This house has a spirit of it's own and it WANTS to bring us together!"

My sweet little fanciful soul, he mused happily.

* * *

They found they had a good solid byre. The roof needed a repair to the thatch but structurally it was sound. There was a granary built on staddle stones and a shed for the fowls.

They paced out the fields, making plans for the future. It looked as though they would have a good crop of hay. Next market day they would go to Dorchester and look for a house cow and a pig, perhaps even buy them, and Steven could stay at the farm to tend them until the wedding. Later they would go in for wool and mutton, it was excellent sheep country.

Sarah had brought some bread, cheese and a flagon of

ale so they sat on the doorstep in the warm April sunshine, surveying their domain. There were apple, pear and plum trees to the west of the house, the blossom like a cloud of pink-tinged snow.

"We can have vegetables over there and on either side of the path I would like to grow flowers for the bees. We CAN have bees, can't we? I used to talk to them when I was a child."

"Of course we will—mmm—lovely honey-comb! We'll need them for the fruit trees, anyhow."

His head pillowed in her lap, they dreamed and planned the afternoon away.

At last, as the shadows lengthened, Steven sighed.

"Well my love, we'd better be getting back. We've a long ride ahead."

They shut their door behind them and mounted the horses, turning before riding off for a final look.

"Happy?" he asked.

"VERY," she answered truthfully, gazing up at him with a contented smile as they rode back to Poole, side by side.

CHAPTER 17

The Wedding

A thrush sang as dawn broke through a light sea mist on the 2nd of June 1589. Sarah woke, confused for a moment to find herself in a strange room, then smiling, stretched like a cat . . . she was in the house of Jane Uvedale's father in the hamlet of Renscombe and today was her wedding day.

Wriggling down into the softness of the bed, she luxuriated in the comfort, letting her thoughts roam. It was early yet and there was plenty of time.

She lay there thinking, "Every morning of my life until today I have woken up alone . . . tomorrow morning Steven's dear, dark, curly head will be lying on the pillow next to mine!" A delicious shiver ran through her and she felt a strange, taut feeling of anticipation in the pit of her stomach.

Yesterday, they had collected armfuls of wild flowers from the hedgerows and Jane and her friends had woven garlands, decorating the little church of St Nicholas at Worth Matravers where the wedding was to be held. They wouldn't let her see—it was to be fresh for her, the bride, today.

Steven had been preparing their cottage at the farm, mending walls, roofs and gates while she had scrubbed the place from top to bottom until it was clean as a daisy. They bought a bed at Dorchester market and carried it home on a cart, padding the carving carefully with straw so it wouldn't be damaged on the rough roads.

Joan from Poole had sent them some pillows and Widow Meryatt had made a beautiful quilt. They were both coming to the wedding and had spent the night at the inn at Corfe. Young Willy was coming too but the younger boy was staying at home with his mother's sister.

There was a tap on her bedroom door.

"Sarah, are you awake?"

"Mmm—come in, do."

"It's going to be a beautiful day. The serving girl has heated the water for your bath, if you are ready, then we will have breakfast before you dress for your wedding . . . how do you feel?"

"Excited, nervous—happy!"

Jane came over to the bed and embraced her friend. There was no question of any "maid and mistress" now—after all, they were to be neighbours from now on.

"You WILL be happy, I know it. Steven is such a caring person, you couldn't be in better hands."

"Not even Hugh's?" asked Sarah mischievously, making Jane blush.

"Oh, I know I am very fond of him. I think he likes me too."

Sarah let out an unladylike shriek.

"LIKES you, he's head over heels in LOVE with you!"

"That's as may be—it's YOUR day today! Come along, miss, the bath water will be tepid," and she held open the door as the girl carried in the buckets.

* * *

Jane brushed the bride's fair curls, gathering them into a plait at the back of her head, circling it with a garland of white fragrant lilies-of-the-valley. She helped Sarah fasten the V-necked bodice, then lifting the kirtle she held it for her to step into, drawing it, rustling, over the chemise and petticoats. The gown had been Jane's gift, the material of the finest ivory silk embroidered with matching lilies and with a short train of satin lined with green taffeta. The pair had worked on it for many hours until the bride-to-be looked like a queen.

"There—you are almost ready." Jane tucked a lace handkerchief into the bride's kirtle, handing her a nosegay of more lilies-of-the-valley and marguerites, fresh and virginal.

The carrier's wagon had been hired for the occasion and

was decked out with ribbons and cushions—the carrier even tying white and green ribbons on his whip.

Sarah descended the stairs where Jane's father was waiting.

"You look like a dream, my dear! Steven is a very lucky man," and giving her his arm, led her to the waggon.

Honeysuckle sweetened the air, its perfume mingling with the lilies in her nosegay as the waggon wound along the lane, travelling the half-mile to the church. Bells rang out across the meadows from the solid square greystone tower, and Sarah thought she would float in the air with happiness.

They turned the final corner, and there was her husband-to-be waiting for her, grey eyes shining, with Ben at his side.

He lifted her reverently, proudly down from the waggon.

"Come, my own love," he said and led her towards the church.

The grotesque stone heads of birds and beasts under the eaves seemed to be smiling benevolently on this happy day as the couple entered the door under Norman arches, centuries old.

Music greeted their arrival. The church was full and every head turned as they began their procession to the altar.

Steven and Sarah led the way, attended by Ben and Jane. The bride and groom looked straight ahead, too aware of the occasion to recognise faces of guests, arriving at last before the Reverend John Kellett and the service began.

The bride was in a haze of happiness, hardly hearing what the vicar was saying, conscious only of Steven at her side. Stealing a glance, she saw he was resplendent in green velvet doublet and hose with a short cloak—a gift from Sir Christopher—and thigh length soft leather boots turned down below the knee. At the same moment he looked down at her and smiled.

It would be impossible to be any happier than I am at this moment, she thought, then was suddenly aware of what the vicar was saying.

"I now pronounce you man and wife together."

Jane came forward, lifting the short veil from the bride's face and Steven stepped forward, holding both her hands.

"My wife," he said simply but the love shone from his eyes and he kissed her warmly but gently on the lips.

The church band struck up the bridal march and they turned to walk down the aisle, acknowledging the smiles of the guests, nodding their heads in greeting.

Near the front, Steven halted and Sarah saw Sir Christopher was there.

Curtsying low, she said, "My Lord, thank you for coming."

"In faith, you are the fairest bride I have seen," he answered with a smile. "May good fortune and health go with you, and you too, Steven."

"Thank you, my Lord," they replied and walked on down the length of the flower-bedecked church.

Sarah suddenly noticed a small, straight figure standing with his mother.

"Willy!" she said, bending to kiss him, her happiness dimmed for a moment at this reminder of sadness, realising what memories the service must have revived for his mother.

Then they reached the church door and she was happy again as they were showered with rose petals by their laughing, excited guests.

* * *

Sir Christopher drank the couple's health.

"I wish I could stay longer," he said "but I'm afraid I must return to Corfe. I have to be in London this week." He drew his ex-secretary to one side. "To tell you the truth, Steven, the Privy Council is becoming concerned over the matter of piracy around our coasts, Dorset—and Studland—in particular so I must make my report as a matter of urgency. He grinned ruefully. "I would have asked you to come with me—but even I wouldn't try to persuade you to leave your lovely bride!"

"Thank you for that, Sir," replied Steven with a half-smile, breathing a sigh of relief.

"Oh, one thing before I go . . . the tall, dark woman soberly dressed with the small boy—is she . . .?"

"Yes, my Lord, Widow Meryatt."

"I guessed as much. Will you introduce me?"

Steven led him over to the table where she sat with Joan.

The widow rose to her feet seeing Sir Christopher approaching, holding herself erect.

He bowed.

"Madam, my sorrows for your sad loss. Is there anything you need?" His dark eyes, full of concern looked deeply into hers. She had been prepared to hate this man, only taking the compensation money for the boys' sake but now, seeing him like this the hard, tight feeling in her chest softened.

"No, thank you my Lord, there is nothing else you can do for us. But . . . we appreciate what you have done already," and she returned his look, recognising the genuine regret in his eyes.

He was turning to leave when a small figure confronted him.

"Are you the man who killed my father?"

The boy's mother put out a hand to restrain him but Sir Christopher waved her away, sitting down on a bench to bring his eyes on a level with the boy's.

"Indirectly, yes," he admitted sadly. "They were my men who fired the sakres and they are being punished. But no amount of punishment will bring back lost lives and I will regret those deaths 'til the end of my days . . . sometimes things happen which are beyond our control, lad. I know you cannot forgive me, but I hope some day you may understand. May God go with you and your mother, and if you ever need help, I hope you will call on me."

The lad looked at him wretchedly.

"We won't need your help, I will look after mother now." He looked away, then continued in a small voice, "I was going to sail with father."

Sir Christopher, deeply touched, put out his arms to the boy.

"Life doesn't always deal us a fair hand, lad. There are things which I too wish for, but which are not to be . . ."

The boy turned back to look at him and with the

perspicacity of children recognised that this great man, too, knew sorrow. His sensitive little heart was moved and he silently went to him, hugging him in his arms.

His mother sighed, saying to the Lord Chancellor, "'Tis a good thing, forgiveness. Hatred rots away the soul like a worm in an apple. I feel better for meeting with you, my Lord."

"And I, likewise," his hand on the boy's shoulder. "Now I must return to Corfe and begin preparations for my journey to London. Farewell."

Taking her hand he lifted it to his lips, kissing it, then ruffling the boy's hair called to his men, mounted his horse and rode back to the castle.

* * *

The guests had gone now and the couple were alone in their cottage having a final drink before retiring.

The long summer's evening turned to violet dusk and an owl called from the wood.

He sat looking at her, rejoicing in her beauty and his good fortune in having her for a bride.

"What are you thinking?" she asked, catching his look.

"I'm thinking what a lucky man I am and that it's been a long day. Are you ready for bed?"

She looked at him blissfully.

"It's been the most wonderful day of my life and there are still a couple of hours to midnight!"

"Come along then, wife!" he challenged, sweeping her off her feet and carrying her laughing up the stairs.

She undressed before him, unembarrassed. This was her man and she wanted to belong to him, to hold nothing back.

Dropping her chemise to the floor she suddenly couldn't bear being apart from him any longer and with a cry ran into his arms, burying her face in his chest.

"Oh my little love," he said thickly, lifting her on to the bed.

In the pale light of the moon they explored each other's bodies, finding excitement in each new discovery until at last, gasping with pleasure they were joined at last and at last together, soaring above the world in timelessness and satiation . . .

* * *

Once, during the night she woke—something was tickling her nose. Thinking it was a spider she opened her eyes wide—and found it was the hair on his chest. The corners of her mouth curled upwards and she snuggled contentedly against him, fitting her form into his long, lean muscular contours, relaxing back into sleep like a puppy.

* * *

It was work as usual next morning. A farm couldn't wait for lovers, but they shared the tasks between them before settling down to breakfast.

"Did you see Sir Christopher talking to Widow Meryatt?" he reflected.

"Mmm. I wondered how she would feel, meeting him like that but they parted on friendly terms—even Willy, although the poor little soul looked rebellious at first."

"Sir Christopher was telling me that something is to be done about the pirates at last," he said, sinking his teeth into crisp brown bread.

She felt a sudden qualm.

"Who is going to do what?" she asked apprehensively.

"Didn't say. Privy Council or some such."

It's nothing to do with us, now, she told herself firmly. All that is finished with—the sea, fighting, now we FARM!

* * *

The time of haymaking came and went and the summer days sped swiftly by. They tended the vegetables in their garden and looked after the stock. The cow had a strong, healthy heifer calf and chickens hatched their eggs. Then, almost imperceptibly, long summer days began to shorten. The weather was still good though and they were content—all was right with their own small world.

Elsewhere, however, things were different . . .

CHAPTER 18

The Reckoning

Steven was aloft in the apple trees dropping fruit carefully into his wife's outstretched apron when there was a shout from the gateway.

"Ahoy there!"

"Ben!" exclaimed Sarah, delighted to see him—then a strange sixth sense hinted that all was not as it should be, although his manner was cheerful enough.

"What brings you here, lad?" called Steven, swinging down from the apple tree, wiping the green lichen from his hands.

"Great news! At last they are taking action against the pirates at Studland! The Privy Council can stand their antics no longer and they've decreed that a stronger line be taken. Can you believe it, they've sent two of Her Majesty's ships, the *Talbot* and the *Unicorn* to Poole and we sail tomorrow!"

"'We?'"

"A call has gone out for able-bodied men who know the surrounding waters and countryside. I have volunteered . . ."

"But they need more men?" finished his cousin, a glint in his eyes.

Then came the question Sarah feared—yet knew was inevitable.

"Aye—are you with us, Steve?"

"Please God, NO!" she breathed, but in his excitement he didn't notice.

"Why, of course, Ben. You know you can count on me! They've had it their own way for long enough, preying on honest mariners . . . but I've a commitment here, too," he considered. "How long do you think it will take?"

"A few days, no more. Today's Monday. You'd be back here by Saturday.

Steven thumped his cousin playfully on the shoulder.

"T'will be like old times, eh?" then looking around for Sarah's approval saw her white, stricken face and suffered a pang of remorse for his thoughtlessness . . . women didn't understand the excitement of battle or the thrill of danger!

"Sarah, my love—don't fret! It won't be like the *Bountifull Gyfte*, she was a sitting duck. We will be armed this time and ready for them!"

Her body trembled. She had felt so safe here with him, life had been so good, but although it wrenched her heart to do so, she knew she must let him go.

"Don't worry about me," she said, putting on a brave face. "I realise what you must do," then forced herself to ask, dreading the answer, "Wh . . . when do you leave?"

He looked enquiringly at Ben.

"We should go right away. The wind's veering to north-east and freshening so we'll have a job to beat against it, leaving the harbour—probably have to warp out. By the same token the pirates will find it difficult getting away from Studland, if we can surprise them. They'll have an on-shore wind."

With nervous hands Sarah hurriedly prepared them some food for the journey back to Poole, whilst Steven saddled Melody.

She stood at the door of their cottage, waving farewell as they rode off together in high spirits.

As soon as they were out of sight she put her hand on her abdomen, thinking, If I'd told him about the babe he wouldn't have gone, but she wanted to share that news with him in a private moment when they were alone together, not, much as she loved him, with Ben present.

* * *

Gulls circled and screamed in the bitterly cold north-easterly which roughened the usually calm anchorage of Studland. Wild white water sucked and plumed around the chalk stacks of Handfast Point and the ships tugged heavily at their anchors.

There were ten of them in the bay—seven men-of-war and three prizes, one of which was the stripped *Salvator of Danzig*. Their sails were furled, masts bare of canvas and men in the equinoxial gales, in fact there were very few signs of activity anywhere on board. The pirates had become complacent, seeing no reason to leave men on watch. After all, were they not an accepted part of the community now, welcomed by mayor and gentry alike?

In the ale-houses of the village though the scene was very different. Around one hundred pirates were making merry, eating, drinking, wenching and doing business with their "customers".

John Newman, the local small-time pirate from Poole was however, smarting with anger.

"I bought they goods, fair and square," he raged. "Seven barrels of beer, ten of oysters and two of bread aboard my *Mary of Poole*. There wuz I, bringing the cargo to Studland for y'all and along comes that danged Vaughan and decides 'ee wants the beer there and then! Fired his danged gun at me, TWICE 'ee did! Then robbed me of me cargo! Jus' 'cos 'ee's a big feller 'ee thinks 'ee can do wot 'ee likes wi' us liddle chaps! D'ye know what? Reckon's 'ee paid me for 'un! Gimmee some danged Brazil nuts! I'll 'ave 'ee one o' these days, see if I don't!"

His colleagues laughed.

"What did 'ee do with they nuts then, John?"

"I took 'un to Dunkirk and sold 'un there. Didn't get much for 'un though, NOW I got a Poole merchant wantin' 'is money or 'is goods, and I b'aint got neither!"

* * *

Not far off in the wind-sculptured sand dunes armed men were hiding, waiting for the signal from their sea-based colleagues. The Poole men had drawn lots. Ben was with the *Talbot*, helping the crew to navigate in strange waters and Steven was with the troops on land.

The plan was for the *Talbot* and the *Unicorn* to head out to sea from Poole, keeping well clear of Studland—then, once past Handfast Point they were to turn and come back inshore around the headland, hopefully taking their quarry unawares. The utmost secrecy was essential to stop the pirates being warned of the plan. The way across the heath was blocked by the foot soldiers and cavalry, spread out to prevent both entrance by spies and escape by the inland route.

Steven hid behind a dune, adrenalin surging, but there was no sign of life from Studland. He looked around cautiously—was that a head over there? He watched and waited holding his breath but it didn't move, then smiling ruefully to himself identified it as the rounded outline of a gorse bush. Come along now, he chided, you are seeing things!

It was bitterly cold in the north-easterly gale and he hunched his shoulders against its force. They had a long wait and there was plenty of time to take note of his surroundings, marvelling at the way shells and stones stood on little pinnacles as the wind eroded the fine dry sand away around them, blowing it in streamers like stinging smoke.

The sun came out but there was no warmth in it. His shadow was thrown in front of him and he watched as it moved almost imperceptibly like a sundial towards a bush. He stayed very still, the sand blowing about him, then blinked as he saw there were now TWO shadows! Turning swiftly, noiselessly on the soft white sand he saw a figure, quite unaware of him creeping through the dunes towards Studland. Melchior Strangeways was trying to warn the pirates!

Oh no you don't! thought Steven, hurling himself forward, tackling the man around the waist, taking him completely by surprise, his cry of fright lost in the teeth of the gale.

The man was quick though, going for a dagger in his copper buckled belt. They rolled over and over grappling, Steven the stronger of the two, but Strangeways managed to grab a handful of sand and threw it into his eyes, temporarily blinding him. Shaking his head and blinking he struck out and luckily for him caught the man full in the face. He felt the cartilage crack beneath his fist and knew the nose had broken. Strangeway's eyes were watering and the tears mixed with the blood spurting from his nose.

"Let I go, I be doin' no harm," he cringed.

"You can stay there where I can be sure of it," muttered Steven twisting the man's arms behind his back and securing them with his belt. He tied his legs together with a kerchief and finished off with a gag leaving him lying out of sight in a hollow while he resumed his watch.

There was a rustle at his side and the captain of the foot soldiers appeared.

"Curnow—that blockhouse on the cliff—is it manned by the pirates?"

"It's supposed to be a defence AGAINST them but it's fallen out of use."

"Is there a gun in it?"

"There is a cannon, I believe."

"By God's beard, if that were to fire, we would have them!"

"There is a track that leads to it. It's exposed, but I think I could get there unobserved."

"Make haste, then. The ships will be here within the half hour."

Steven slipped away from the heathland making his way up a little combe that led to the cliff top. It was in full view of the tavern but he kept a low profile, bending double and using what cover there was.

The door of the tavern opened and a man came out. Steven froze in his tracks. The man staggered away behind a tree, answering a call of nature, then unconcernedly returned to the alehouse.

Steven had almost gained the cover of the blockhouse when a terrific gust of wind caught him. Off balance he staggered and the edge of the cliff gave way under his feet, tumbling and bouncing into sea below. He felt himself going with it—it was like one of those nightmares when you feel yourself falling over a cliff, grasping at grass which pulls away and you wake up with a jump—but this was real!

Frantically he grabbed a gorse branch, wincing as the spines bit into his flesh. Looking up, he saw it was in flower.

"Kissing is still in fashion!" he murmured stupidly, thinking of Sarah, and hung full length over the cliff feeling the sinews cracking in his arms.

Painfully, inch by inch he pulled himself back, scrabbling for a foothold, feeling the gorse roots beginning to give. Sweat poured from him, turning icy in the wind then with a supreme effort he swung his leg over the top and hauled himself to safety, lying there breathing heavily and looking at the sky . . .

No time for this! he thought taking a deep breath, pulling himself together, getting to his feet and running the last few yards to the blockhouse. Please God it's not locked!

The door gave to a thrust of his shoulder and he found himself inside. There was a cannon pointing out to sea. Putting his back against it he gave several mighty heaves and managed to manoeuvre it around until it was aimed at the *Queen of Padstowe*. There was shot piled in a corner and a box marked POWDER. He tugged at the lid but nothing happened—it was locked!

"Hell's teeth," he gritted looking around for something to open it. Finding an iron bar rusty but sound, he prayed Let's hope I don't make a spark, easing the bar under the lock and carefully levering it open. The catch broke and he fell forward on to the box, sucking his hand which was still pitted with gorse spears.

The powder was stored in leather pouches. Slitting them open carefully with his knife he loaded the cannon, just managing to prime it ready to fire when a glorious sight appeared—the *Talbot* and the *Unicorn* sailed into view around Handfast Point and headed towards the pirate ships, firing sakres across their bows.

So unexpected was the attack that the pirates were completely disorganised. Men came pouring out of the tavern in disarray, buckling on swords and pulling on boots.

A roar went up from the land-based troops and cavalry. "Put up your weapons—you are surrounded!"

Ben, on the *Talbot* rowed ashore with the crew, leaping into battle with his sword, fighting bravely. Sparks flew as weapon clashed against weapon then came a cry, "Look to your left, lad!" and turning swiftly he avoided a blow from one of Vaughan's men who uttered a gurgling yell as he was run through by the owner of the voice.

Glancing to see who had saved him he recognised the pirate Clinton Atkinson, his friend from Studland days and their eyes met and locked.

"I never did like Vaughan's crowd!" chuckled Clinton wryly, then seeing he was outnumbered surrendered his sword to Ben, who took it reluctantly.

How ironic, he thought, the one man who befriended me!

* * *

Steven, in the blockhouse, recognised John Piers and his men as they ran down the shore to a boat, pushing it into the water and rowing out towards the *Queen of Padstowe*.

"I hope you work and don't explode!" he said to the cannon, sighting along the barrel, patting it affectionately and applying the linstock.

With a roar that deafened him the cannon fired, the shot hitting the sea alongside Piers, overturning his boat and upsetting him and his men into the water.

"WELL—that wasn't bad for such a rough aim!" muttered Steven thankfully, sinking to the ground with relief.

The foot soldiers were on the scene now and waded in, guns at the ready. Piers came up gasping and raised his hands in defeat. The unexpected attack from the apparently deserted blockhouse had completely unnerved him.

The surprise element of the encounter had been the winning trump card. One hundred pirates and seven barques defeated by two of Her Majesty's ships with a handful of cavalry and foot troops!

The pirate captains were rounded up and handcuffed.

"Get them loaded into carts!" shouted the Commander and they were unceremoniously bundled aboard.

"I've gold," hissed Piers to Steven who was holding the horse's head and supervising the loading. "Let me slip away and 'tis yours!"

Steven wiped his mouth with the back of his hand, looking scornfully at the pirate.

"'Tis justice for you this time, gold or no gold," and turned away.

Ben hurried over to the *Salvator of Danzig* which lay on her side on the sand. Casting his eye over her he saw several planks were sprung but the damage didn't look beyond repair. Her master will be relieved to get her back, he thought. The sale of Vaughan's goods will pay for the damage!

* * *

The pirates were taken in the carts to Corfe Castle where a special sessions of the Dorset Commissioners was held.

There was to be no mercy—the sentence was hanging by the neck at Studland "for the terrifying of others"—and a few weeks later they were returned there in the same carts, bumping along the track on top of the chalk downland.

Sawing and hammering disturbed the still air as gibbets were set up on the beach and crowds gathered to watch; pirates executions were always popular.

Those condemned were John Piers, William Vaughan, Clinton Atkinson and four others. Piers' sickly complexion was paler than ever and death was written on his face before the noose was put around his neck. Flamboyant in death as in life the others played to the gallery, Vaughan swearing colourful oaths at "justice", calling down a curse on his captors and spitting at the hangman. The last to be hung while the others still twitched on their fine Bridport ropes was Clinton Atkinson, who gave away his finery to the onlookers.

"I must apologize for my means of dying," he said. "I hope I do it well, but it's something I've never done before and have had little practice!"

The crowds roared their approval, applauding him as he stepped to the gibbet. Then, as the tide turned, the last of the condemned men put his head in the noose and was jerked off his feet, toes dancing a macabre dance on the waves . . .

Epilogue

The four year old ran past the beehives, up the garden path through the bed of foxgloves and forget-me-nots and into his father's arms.

"I can do it, I can do it!" he cried putting his chubby hands behind his back, playing the age-old game. "Ship sails!"

"Sails fast," responded his father.

"How many men on board?" queried the boy holding out his hands in front of him, fists clenched.

"Er . . . two?"

"YES, YES," shouted the lad gleefully, opening his fists and displaying two round pebbles—"Me and you,father, sailing away on the sea together!"

Smiling tenderly at her two 'men' Sarah came from the farmhouse pantry where rows of preserves, jams and chutneys lined the shelves. The spirit of adventure there already, and he so young! Ah well, it was in the blood—but she would have them to herself for a few years yet, please God. Everything she desired in the world was here—Steven, her beloved son, their farm, and in a few months another child, a girl this time, perhaps . . .?

* * *

A rider came trotting along the hawthorn fringed lane to the house.

"It's Uncle Ben," called the child happily. "Hello Uncle Ben. Will you play 'Ship Sails' with us?"

Dismounting, Ben kissed the child then called, "Steven, Sarah, I've come from Poole. What do you think—the *Bountifull Gyfte* is up for sale again! I was thinking of buying her. It's a wonderful opportunity—would you consider a partnership, Steven?"

The man looked around his farm and family.

"Ben, if it's money you need I'll put up my share. We've done well these past few years, but as to sailing with you —everything I've ever wanted is HERE, lad."

Sarah's heart leapt. So he felt that way too! All her secret fears that he was staying there on her account were groundless!

Ben smiled crookedly.

"I rather thought you'd say that. A 'sleeping' partner will suit me fine. Oh—and young Willy Meryatt wants to sail with me. I've said he can, he has the makings of a fine seaman and the *'Gyfte* was his father's vessel, after all." He looked away, shuffling his feet awkwardly, fiddling with the horse's reins and searching for the right words.

"Er . . . by the way, I was thinking of taking the ship to Plymouth and making that my home port." He looked at his cousin with embarrassment. "You see, there's a girl there I'm rather fond of. She has a fine house, left to her by her parents and I'm—er—thinking of making her my bride." Blushing, he fingered his collar.

Running forward, Sarah gave him a big hug and Steven gripped his shoulder saying, "At last, we thought you'd NEVER settle down! We're delighted, lad. If you are half as happy as we are you'll be over the moon! Come inside and have a drink to celebrate—we've a fine Gascon wine—compliments of Francis Hawley!"

* * *

Away in the woods behind the house, a yaffingale swooped and chuckled . . .

FOOTNOTE

On 12th December 1590 a grant of pardon was issued, and Wal Partridge's life was spared.

In November 1591 Sir Christopher Hatton died, aged 51. He never married and his adopted son William inherited Corfe Castle—but that is another story!

PLACE NAMES

Modern Spelling	
Blanchinwell	Belchalwell
Branksea	Brownsea
Cales, the	Sandbanks
Fursey	Furzey Island
Haven House	Flag Farm
Kimbridge	Kimmeridge
St Helen's	Green Island
Shipmans Pool	Chapmans Pool
Sandwyche	Swanage
Woodberry	Woodbury

GLOSSARY

Barbican	walled courtyard
Culverin	long cannon
Destrier	war horse
Falconet	light cannon
Farthingale	undergarment to make the skirt stand out
Fustian	fabric of cotton and flax
Galleas	large boat propelled by oars
Harquebus	portable gun, supported on a hooked rest
Jupon	doublet emblazoned with coat of arms, worn over armour
Kirtle	underskirt
Linstock	stick with a match or lint at the end, to light a fuse
Marchpane	marzipan
Moiety	legal term for 'half', or of two parts
Parrel	wooden bearings surrounding masts
Sakre	piece of ordnance with three and a half inch bore, firing a shot of five and a half pounds
Stomacher	long, inverted triangular-shaped fill-in for the bodice, elaborately embroidered
Yaffingale	green woodpecker